#3

JUNIOR HIGH

THE DAY THE EIGHTH GRADE RAN THE SCHOOL

JUNIOR HIGH

Junior High Jitters
Class Crush
The Day the Eighth Grade Ran the School

THE DAY THE EIGHTH GRADE RAN THE SCHOOL

Kate Kenyon

SCHOLASTIC INC.
New York Toronto London Auckland Sydney

ISBN 0-590-41818-1

12 11 10 9 8 7 6 5 2/9

Printed in the U.S.A. 01

First Scholastic printing, March 1987

Chapter 1

Nora Ryan was having a perfectly rotten day and it wasn't even half over.

At the bus stop earlier that morning, a car whizzing too close to the curb had splashed mud on her favorite jeans, the ones that had taken a whole year to break in so they fit just right.

"Did you see that?" Nora had asked Jennifer Mann, her best friend. "That car aimed right for me. He knew he was throwing water all over me. I do *not* lead a charmed life."

Nora, who was usually prepared for any emergency short of a National Alert, didn't even have a Kleenex with her. Jen lent her friend her last tissue. Nora wiped off the dirt the best she could. That was the first thing that happened.

The next thing was when Nora and Jennifer were standing outside on the front steps of Cedar Groves Junior High before classes started. Even though it was cold and a mean, drizzly rain was falling, most of the eighth-graders congregated on the front steps. It was a tradition.

Suddenly a sharp gust of wind tore around the corner, ripping Nora's raincoat hood from her head. Nora grabbed for her hood, clumsily dropping her notebook. The wind fanned the pages of her notebook wildly, and then gave an extra big puff that sent Nora's history assignment flying past the parked school buses.

"Nora!" Jen had cried. She started to run after the sailing papers, but Nora pulled her back. By the time the two of them reached the school bus lane, Nora reasoned, her homework would be halfway to the next county.

"Four hours worth of work," she said dismally, as the bell rang. "Gone with the wind. Literally."

If Nora Ryan weren't so sensible and practical, she would have gone back home, crawled into bed, and pulled the covers over her head. But Nora planned to be a doctor someday, and her sensible, practical mind refused to accept the notion that there was some kind of conspiracy against her. Yet her day did not improve once she was indoors.

Because she didn't have her history assignment, Mr. Robards kept Nora after class for an explanation. He was sympathetic as Nora told him about the Ill Wind that blew her homework away. Mr. Robards granted Nora an extra two days to redo her assignment. Nora was grateful but she was also very late to lunch.

She ran to the cafeteria, just in time to be the last person in the serving line. She was starving. Would this day ever *end*?

Nora leaned against the bile-green wall and stared blankly out the window. No point in hurrying now. She looked over at the seventh-graders, whose tables crowded the serving line, as they crammed down their food. It was truly a nauseating spectacle, but then she didn't expect much from seventh-graders.

Jennifer would be saving her a seat at the center table usually reserved for eighth-graders, well away from the seventh-graders and a safe distance from the know-it-all ninth-graders. Jennifer and the others were probably through eating and would now be having a fascinating discussion, while Nora was still stuck in the lunch line.

Nora grabbed a steel tray, slammed a handful of flatware on it, and pushed it along the rails so hard, her tray rammed into the tray of the boy in front of her.

"Sorry," Nora mumbled. Fortunately she hadn't pinched his fingers.

The boy turned around to see who had sent his tray skidding into the salad section.

Marc Johnson was a brand-new student at Cedar Groves Junior High, recently transferred from California. Nora gawked at him in history, along with all the other girls in her class who stared at the new boy in open admiration. Marc had sun-streaked blond hair worn a little longer than was fashionable and a tan that made everyone else at Cedar Groves look as if they'd been underground most of their lives. He smiled at Nora, a generous reaction in view of the fact that she had knocked his tray halfway down the line.

For one insane instant, Nora forgot about lunch and fervently wished she were tall and willowy and had long blonde hair. Ordinarily she didn't mind her curly brown hair, and as for being short — well, Jennifer loyally called her "petite," but sometimes her height was a pain. Stupid little things like the time last year when a teacher told her to stand up and Nora replied that she *was* standing. She could still hear the laughter.

Marc took the pasta salad the server handed him, flashing the woman his winning smile. Not only was he gorgeous, but he seemed genuinely *nice*, a rare quality among eighth-grade boys. Probably a vegetarian, too. Nora was sure Marc was into backpacking and bicycling, all that healthy Californian stuff.

"Salad plate, please," Nora told the server, when it was finally her turn.

"Out of salads," the woman informed her. "He got the last one." She pointed to Marc, who was picking up what appeared to be the last piece of carrot cake.

The server gave her a plate containing two tired-looking hot dogs in a pool of gummy beans. Nora took the plate without a fuss. She would eat the baked beans and the dried-up scalloped potatoes and ignore the nitrate-loaded hot dogs. Nora had learned a long time ago to eat foods that were nutritious without making a big deal out of it.

Somehow it seemed fitting that she would be handed a hot dog today.

"What *kept* you so long?" Jennifer asked when Nora sat down. "I was about to call out a search party."

Nora began wolfing down baked beans in a manner that would have put the seventh-graders in the shade. "Mr. Robards made me stay after class. By the time I got here, I was last. They were out of salads and carrot cake, so I was forced to take this or nothing." She stopped gobbling, suddenly realizing the beans were congealing before her very eyes. "Yuck! Will you look at this roll, Jen? Did a gorilla stomp on this or what? Honestly, the food at the end of the line is gross."

"It's not much better at the front of the line," Lucy Armanson complained. She sat slumped before her tray, one hand entwined in her shiny black Afro, idling her fork back and forth through something that could have been either tuna salad or a tennis ball left out in the rain.

Jennifer had finished her lunch and was scribbling something in her notebook. "If I had known you were going to be so late, I would have saved you my dessert," she said sympathetically.

"Thanks," Nora said. "But on a day like today, one piece of carrot cake wouldn't help much."

"What's wrong?" Jennifer had never seen her normally bubbly friend so morose.

"What's right?" Nora pointed to Jennifer's open notebook. "Another one of your missionary letters?"

Jennifer smoothed her dark hair behind one ear and regarded Nora with round hazel eyes. "It's an adoption notice for this week's newspaper. Four dogs and six cats whose time is almost up. I'm supposed to write an appealing notice to get people's attention. Maybe some of the animals will be adopted before . . . before this Saturday."

Nora knew Jennifer meant before the animals were put to sleep. It continually amazed her how one person devoted so much time to caring. When Jennifer wasn't working at the animal shelter, or reading to the elderly residents of the nursing home, or baking cookies for sick friends, she was writing letters in behalf of starving children in Africa, endangered animals, homeless people, and other causes. Despite her shyness, Jennifer got out there and fought for the rights of the downtrodden and the underdogs. Nora admired her friend for that.

Now Jennifer pushed away her notebook. "This notice is anything but appealing," she said. "I can't seem to write today."

From across the table, Denise Hendrix gave up on her lunch with a sigh.

"You, too?" Nora asked.

"I *was* hungry," Denise said. "But lately the food hasn't been very appetizing." Denise, who was blonde, beautiful, and the heiress to the Denise Cosmetics fortune, had grown up in Europe where she attended boarding schools. Recently, her father had brought his family back to Cedar Groves, his old hometown. While everyone else in the Hendrix family was putting down roots, Denise was still suffering from culture shock.

"What is *wrong* with everybody today?" Tracy Douglas checked her lip gloss in the mirror of her compact, then snapped the compact shut. "The food isn't that bad."

"Yes, it is," Nora contradicted her. "But it isn't just the food."

"What do you mean?" Lucy asked, sitting up for the first time all lunch period.

Nora poked disdainfully at the beans turning to cement on her plate. "The ladies in the cafeteria don't even *try* to make our lunches appetizing. But it's not really their fault."

"Whose fault is it?" Jennifer asked.

"The school's." The answer slipped out before Nora fully understood the importance of her words. But then the idea caught hold and grew. "This school is positively falling *apart*. Feel under the table — the gum hasn't been scraped from under it in *ages*. The same notices have been on the bulletin board by the office since 1974. There's one toilet in the girl's room that hasn't flushed right since the beginning of the year. Need I go on?" She picked up her fork and rapped it against the rim of her tray for emphasis. "Everything about this school is dull, including the teachers. And they're supposed to make learning *interesting* for us."

"Our homeroom teacher, Mr. Mario,

looks like the man in the commercial for iron-poor blood," Jennifer put in. "I get tired just listening to him drone through the roll."

"He's that way in Italian, too," Denise put in. She was the only person in their group taking Italian. The others took French, a requirement, but because Denise had been educated in France and Switzerland, she already spoke French fluently.

"How do they expect us to learn when they all sound like they are reading the *Congressional Record*?" Nora pointed out.

"Maybe our teachers have the damp miseries," Jennifer suggested.

"The whats?" Tracy asked. Jennifer smiled at her. She liked the boy-crazy blonde girl, even though Nora thought Tracy was a space cadet.

"Damp miseries." Jen indicated the windows, where sheets of rain drooled down the panes. "That's what Jeff says this weather gives him. I think he's reading *Moby Dick* again."

Jeff Crawford was the Manns' housekeeper. Jennifer's mother had died when she and her brother Eric were very young, and none of the housekeepers Mr. Mann hired had worked out until Jeff came along. He was such a part of the family, Jennifer didn't know what she'd do if he ever left.

Lucy Armanson picked up her tray. "This is a damp miseries kind of a day if I ever saw one."

The other girls took their trays to the dishwashing area of the cafeteria, leaving Nora and Jennifer alone.

"You know, Jen, we haven't even scratched the surface of all the things wrong with this school," Nora said. "I bet if we made a list, it would be a mile long. Maybe two miles."

Jennifer turned to a clean page in her notebook and began writing. " 'Gum under tables, rotten lunches, broken toilet in girls' room,' " she read aloud as she jotted down each item. "That's three. Hardly a mile, do you think?"

"Jen, you're not taking this seriously. If *we* don't care about the way this place is run, *they* sure aren't going to care." She waved in the general direction of the main office.

Jennifer stared at her friend. "That's a pretty strong statement, Nora. In fact, it's practically an accusation."

Nora spun Jennifer's notebook around so she could see it, too. "Put down boring teachers — no, we'd better break them down into classes. The list will have more impact that way. Dull assemblies, pep rallies without pep . . . we could go on forever."

"How about the principal's announcements over the P.A. every morning? They've gotten so boring I don't even listen anymore," Jen said.

"Snore-City," Nora agreed. "Write that down."

"What else?"

Nora was momentarily distracted by a sunny-haired boy taking his tray to the back. She leaned forward and whispered, "There goes that Marc Johnson. You know, the new guy in history? He's just what this school needs — a breath of fresh air. I think he's so cute."

"So does every other girl in the eighth grade," Jennifer said wryly.

"Don't you like him?"

"I don't know." Jennifer was as interested in boys as Nora, but she was more reserved in judging people. "I don't really know him."

"Neither do I, but I like what I've seen so far."

Jennifer watched Marc join the boys at his table. She had to admit that he certainly behaved better than Mitch Pauley or that geeky Jason Anthony. Jason imagined himself some sort of a red-haired daredevil, zooming down the hall on his skateboard, an act definitely forbidden in school, yet he managed to get away with it. If Jennifer ever had to describe the most immature, irritating, disgusting eighth-grade boy in the entire world to the police for some reason, the police artist would sketch a portrait of Jason Anthony, and he'd be behind bars in no time.

"The trouble with the boys around here," Nora was saying, "is that they're all so *frantic*. Not Marc. He's cool. Laid-back. People from California are like that. It comes from a healthy life-style — hiking in the mountains, surfing, eating right — "

" — falling asleep in class," Jennifer added.

"What?"

"Marc is in my algebra class. He fell asleep yesterday and didn't wake up until the bell rang."

"Are you sure it was Marc?" Nora frowned. "He's too mellow to do things like that. That's more Jason's style."

"Mellow he might be, but he still went beddy-bye in class. It was Marc all right. No way can you mistake Marc for Jason. That's impossible."

"Well." Nora fished around for an excuse to make for Marc. "Maybe he's having trouble adjusting to the climate change."

Jennifer grinned. She could see her friend was crazy about the new boy. "He probably has the damp miseries."

Nora wrinkled her nose at what was left of her lunch. "Don't we all?"

Chapter 2

Over the phone that evening, Nora and Jennifer expanded the Gripe List until it was almost two whole pages. Jennifer remarked she had never realized how many things were wrong with their school.

"This is just the tip of the iceberg," Nora said. "Imagine how long this list would be if we added the gripes of *all* the kids in Cedar Groves."

"Nora, what are we going to do with this list?" Jennifer wanted to know.

"I know what I'd *like* to do with it. Have it printed on the front page of the Cedar Groves *Sun*, right where the principal would be sure to see it." She sighed. "I guess we won't do anything with it. Are you going to watch the TV movie tonight?"

"The one about the woman with all the foster children? I wouldn't miss it. But first I have to do my homework."

Nora moaned. "You had to remind me!

I have to make up that assignment that blew across town today. I got so involved in our Gripe List, I forgot all about it."

"Anything I can do to help?" Jennifer offered.

"Thanks, but it's the kind of paper I have to do by myself. It shouldn't take me too long, since I still have my notes."

"Well, I'd better let you go so you can get started. What are you wearing tomorrow?" Jennifer asked. This was part of their evening routine. They talked to each other every single night over the phone, even after being together most of the day in school.

If Nora was wearing pants, Jennifer would wear pants, too. On the days Jennifer decided to wear a skirt and sweater, Nora wore a skirt, too, so that they were always dressed — if not exactly alike — then compatibly.

Jennifer thought, as she often did, how her friendship with Nora Ryan went beyond mere friendship. It was a feeling she couldn't put into words. She couldn't even express it in the diary she recorded the day's events in every night. She and Nora were closer than best friends, closer than sisters, closer maybe than twins. Jennifer didn't know much about the relationship between twins, and she only had a younger brother. But Nora had an older sister, and

Jennifer knew that Nora and Sally didn't always get along. She and Nora rarely fought, although they did have differences of opinion.

"Nora?" she said. "I asked what you were wearing tomorrow."

"Sorry." Nora sounded distant. "I was thinking about my wonderful day. I'll probably wear mud-spattered jeans, if tomorrow is anything like today was."

Jennifer said helpfully, "The odds are against having two rotten days in a row."

"I certainly hope so."

Jennifer woke up early the next morning, thinking about that day in kindergarten many years ago when she became friends with Nora.

She had noticed Nora from the first day. How could she not? Nora was the only kid in kindergarten who could print her name without making any mistakes. Jennifer had trouble with N's. She printed them backward and there were *four* in her name. In school, Jennifer sat beside Nora, admiring the other girl's perfect N's.

Nora looked over at Jennifer's paper. Embarrassed, Jennifer put her hands over it, but she knew Nora had seen her backward N's. But Nora didn't make fun of her. Instead, she handed Jennifer a crayon. It had hardly been used; the paper was still on the crayon. All of Jennifer's crayons were ratty and worn down to nubs.

"This is my favorite crayon," Nora told her. "Blue-green. It colors the prettiest water. I want you to have it."

Jennifer still had that crayon, in a box of keepsakes. The paper was faded and the crayon was a little lopsided from getting soft each summer. With Nora's gift, the blue-green crayon, she had practiced making N's that year, and by the time kindergarten was over, Jennifer's N's were marvels to behold, and she and Nora Ryan were the best of friends.

Jennifer treasured her friendship with Nora, as she treasured Nora's gift. Losing her mother so young had made Jennifer a thoughtful, sensitive girl. She didn't take friendship for granted.

Downstairs, she found Jeff Crawford breaking eggs into a bowl, preparing to make his special scrambled eggs.

"Jeff, I have a big favor to ask," she said.

He cracked the last egg and tossed the shell into the trash before replying. "You know, there are two sentences a person should never utter before breakfast. One is, 'Guess who's coming to stay with us for six months?' And the other is, 'I have a big favor to ask.' Whatever happened to 'Good morning, Jeff?' "

Jennifer giggled. Jeff was such an old

softie. This morning he wore over his sweater and khakis a canvas apron that said: LIFE IS UNCERTAIN. EAT DESSERT FIRST — a present from his girl friend Debby. Jennifer often wondered if Jeff and Debby would get married. So far, he seemed perfectly content running the Mann house. She hoped he'd stay forever, even though it was a selfish thought. But seeing his big body, gray hair, and blue eyes every morning made her feel safe.

"Good morning, Jeff," she parroted. "Now can I ask the big favor? Would you drop this off at the newspaper office this morning?" She handed him her animal adoption notice.

Jeff said he would. Jennifer ate breakfast with her brother Eric, who caught a later bus to elementary school. Before leaving, Jennifer wrapped up the last piece of Jeff's terrific banana loaf for Nora. Jennifer knew her friend would be rushed, after having worked on her history report most of the night, and would only have time for a bowl of granola. The banana bread would be a nice surprise.

"How did you know I'd be starving?" Nora asked Jennifer at the bus stop. She ate the banana bread without even putting her books down.

Steve Crowley sauntered over and made

loud chewing noises. "Looks delish. Why don't you share, Nora?" His dark brown hair was falling over his blue eyes.

She finished the last bite, licking the ends of her fingers with gusto. "All gone. Besides, Jennifer brought it for me."

Steve turned to Jennifer, making his big eyes look puppy-dog sad. "How come you didn't bring me any?"

Jennifer giggled. She and Nora had known Steve since kindergarten — he was okay. "Sorry. I'll bring two pieces next time."

"Well, okay. Hey — what's this?" Steve grabbed at some papers sticking out of Jennifer's notebook.

"Don't touch that!" Jennifer cried, but it was too late. Steve yanked the papers out of her reach.

"Wow, this is great!" he declared, reading the heading. "A Gripe List!" He looked first at Jennifer and then at Nora. "This has all the hallmarks of a Nora Ryan Scheme. Am I right?"

"Never mind," Nora said tartly. "Just give it back."

"I think I'll hang on to it a while longer, if you don't mind."

"We *do* mind," Nora said. "It's personal property."

But Steve kept the list. When the bus arrived, Steve took the back seat as he always did and circulated the Gripe List around the boys who sat with him.

"Everything that's on here is absolutely true," Steve said.

Mitch Pauley, the captain of the football team, who was reading the list, agreed. "You know, we ought to let our teachers know just how we feel. All of us."

Steve bounced in the seat with excitement. "We could incite a riot — no, wait, I've got it! We'll stage a revolution! A Gripe Revolution!" Steve shouted. Everyone around him took up the battle cry.

In the seat in front of Steve and Mitch, Jennifer looked at Nora. She knew what her friend was thinking. A Gripe Revolution! How did their simple little list get out of hand so fast?

The Gripe Revolution swept the halls of Cedar Groves Junior High like wildfire. Someone, probably Steve, had the Gripe List run off on the mimeograph and copies of it were circulated everywhere. Nora's original list was now four pages and growing as other eighth-grade malcontents added their own gripes. The classes were filled with dour, complaining students who waved the Gripe List around like a banner.

Most of the teachers tried to ignore the grousing. In Nora's homeroom, Tommy Ryder pretended to fall asleep when the principal began his daily drone of announcements. Soon the other boys were mimicking him. Tommy was the class flirt and the boys in his class thought he was a success with girls.

"That was a wasted effort," Nora said to Jen. "Mr. Mario hardly noticed half the class sounded like buzzsaws. He thinks we're as dull as he is, I guess."

But in phys. ed., Ms. Scott squelched the groans that accompanied her order for them to begin exercising with an earsplitting blast of her whistle.

"I don't know about this," Jennifer said to Nora in the locker room. "Somehow it doesn't seem very constructive. I mean, I write letters and sign petitions all the time. But this — this *grumbling* seems like a dumb way to go about changing things."

Nora didn't say anything. In a way, she had started the Gripe Revolution, though no one but Jennifer knew that for sure. Part of her hoped the whole affair would die a natural death. But a smaller, more insistent part of her wondered if the Bellyache Rebellion, as she privately called it, would turn into something that kids attending Cedar Groves Junior High would talk about in the years to come. How a student named Nora Ryan revolutionized the whole system and rescued future classes from middle school mediocrity.

A few evenings later, Nora's older sister asked her to go with her to the mall. Sally, who was studying to be a professional dancer, declared she had worn out yet another pair of toe shoes and could not live without a new pair. Since Sally had begun taking classes at the local university, she had become a real human being, Nora decided. Over the years, they'd had some knock-down-drag-outs, but now her sister almost treated her as an equal.

At the mall, Sally went into Encore, a dance attire shop, and Nora walked up to the counter at the Orange Bowl, suddenly thirsty for an orange drink. And then she saw *him*. Marc Johnson, standing right next to the napkin dispenser. Nora looked down at what she had on: a grubby T-shirt and her crummiest pair of jeans. Why was it whenever she looked her absolute *worst*, she was certain to run into a boy she liked?

The guy behind the counter suddenly demanded, "What'll you have?"

Marc's face lit up as he recognized her. He came over, bringing his drink. "Hi," he said. "You're — wait a minute, don't tell me — Nora!"

Nora paid for her drink and unzipped a straw. He was so blond! So handsome! And so *close* to her! "That's right. And you're Marc. We have history together.

How do you like Cedar Groves so far?"

"You know, I didn't like it much at first," he admitted. "But the last few days have been really wild. I think this Gripe Revolution is the greatest!"

"You do?"

"Oh, yeah. I'm really getting into it. I added a whole bunch of stuff to the Gripe List about how poor the system is for transfer students. Mix-ups in the office, lost transfer records — you name it."

Nora knew people in California were naturally outgoing and friendly, but she had no idea it would be this easy talking to Marc. Any girl in the entire school would willingly walk to the ends of the earth for him. But he was talking to *her*, Nora Ryan, congratulating the anonymous "cool dude" who thought up the idea of a Gripe List.

Nora was never sure whether it was the orange drink she gulped too fast or the head-spinning nearness of Marc that caused her to confess that *she* was the one who originated the Gripe List.

"Really?" he exclaimed. "Far out! Then you started the whole Gripe Revolution!"

"Yeah, I guess I did," Nora said weakly. "Although Steve Crowley really gave it the name."

Marc leaned closer, nearly causing Nora to stop breathing, and said, conspiratorially, "What's your next move, Nora?"

"My next move?"

"You know, the next step in your plan," he pursued.

"Plan?"

"You must have a plan — what's the point of everyone griping? Suppose the teachers ask us about it — what will you *say*?"

Slowly it came to Nora that he was not talking about kissing, something that was very much on her mind at that moment, but about the Gripe Revolution. "I'm going to say — " Nora thought woozily. Say what? What *was* the solution to the endless problems at Cedar Groves? And then she knew. It was so obvious she couldn't imagine why she hadn't thought of it sooner.

"I'm going to tell the teachers and the administration that the eighth grade could run the school better than they do," she proclaimed.

"Wow!" Marc said. "Far out!"

Yes, it was, Nora agreed silently. But of course this was just talk. A foolish idea bandied about between two people over an orange drink. Nothing would come of it.

"All right, class, today we're going to continue our unit on the American Revolution. Get out your books."

Mr. Robards' announcement was instantly greeted with a chorus of groans.

Mr. Robards wasn't having any of it today. He slammed the textbook closed and said, "All right, people. I've put up with your sour faces and whining all week and I want to end it now. What do you want me to do? Stop teaching?"

"That's an idea!" some smart-aleck in the back said. Jennifer turned in her seat, suspecting that Jason Anthony was the source.

Mr. Robards ignored him. "I've seen copies of this famous Gripe List floating around. I understand your complaints. But what do you want us to *do* about them?" For once, the class was attentive. "Come on," he urged. "I'm giving you a chance to talk over this situation. I'm willing — eager, even — to listen."

There followed an outpouring of complaints that Mr. Robards halted by raising his hand. "I don't want to hear any more of your grievances — I've heard them all week. Do you have any recommendations?"

"Why don't we all just quit?" came the smart-aleck from the back.

"How about an all-day study hall for teachers and students?" suggested Mitch Pauley. It was a well-known fact he would rather be on a playing field than in class any day.

"And do what?" Mr. Robards threw back at him.

Mitch shrugged. "Anything we want."

"Does anyone have any *feasible* suggestions?" Mr. Robards pressed. "Does anyone know what the *problem* is or do you just want to get out of studying today by making stupid remarks?"

Mia Stevens raised her hand, waggling her neon-tipped fingers. Today, the class punk had her spiked hair streaked green to match her nail polish. "Mr. Robards, the problem is that we're not interested in learning anymore because you guys don't make learning very interesting."

Andy Warwick, her boyfriend since seventh grade, piped, "Way to go, Mia!" He clapped, jangling the chains he wore around one wrist.

"Okay," Mr. Robards conceded. "Now we're getting somewhere."

Marc Johnson stood up. "Can I say something?" Mr. Robards nodded. "In California, where I used to live, I went to an alternative school — "

"A what school?" Jason Anthony broke in. "An alternative to what?"

"Be quiet!" Amy Williams slapped his desk. "Let him finish."

Marc flashed her his easy smile and continued. "Well, see, in my old school we used to do neat stuff, like choose our own curriculum. The teachers there were really cool. They gave us lots of freedom. And if we had a problem, they'd let us work it out ourselves."

Nora scribbled a hasty note to Jennifer and passed it to her. Jennifer unfolded the paper and read, "Isn't he smart? He is so *deep.*"

"Just what are you suggesting, Marc?" Mr. Robards asked.

"Well, I think we ought to do like those minutemen guys did during the Revolution," Marc said. "Their whole purpose in fighting the British was to have a chance to run the country themselves. Right?"

Mr. Robards looked like he was getting a tension headache. "Are you suggesting that we let you *students* run the school?"

"Yeah!" Marc said. "You know, like a real democracy!"

"That's — quite a suggestion," Mr. Robards said. "A little radical, but the most sensible one made so far. Good thinking, Marc, to tie in what you are learning in history to today's problems."

"Oh, it wasn't my idea," Marc said modestly. "*She* was the one who thought of it." He swung around, pointing directly at Nora Ryan.

Chapter 3

"I could have *died,*" Nora said, burying her face in her pillow. The school day was over, at long last. Jennifer had come home with Nora to give her "moral support" after Marc had dropped his bombshell in history class, and they were sitting in Nora's bedroom. "Everybody was *staring* at me."

"I know," Jennifer said. "I was one of them. Nora, have you lost your mind? Telling Marc Johnson you think the kids could do a better job of running the school than the grown-ups."

"Well, we *could.*" Nora sat up again to defend herself. "If somebody gave us the chance. When I said that to Marc, I didn't think he'd get up in middle of class and announce it to the whole world."

"And tell everybody it was *your* idea. At least he gave you credit."

Nora hugged the pink calico cat cushion

that Jen had made her. "Jen, what do you think is going to happen?"

Jennifer shrugged. "Mr. Robards thought Marc's suggestion was good. He said he'd bring it up at the staff meeting this afternoon."

"You have to admit Marc made our case sound very convincing," Nora said, rather smugly. "Marc single-handedly did more for the cause than the Gripe List and the Gripe Revolution together. He's awfully smart and yet not show-offy like Jason and some of the others."

"I'd call getting up in class and demanding to let the kids run the school pretty nervy." Jennifer kicked off her shoes and stretched out on Nora's bed. "What really happened last night at the mall?"

"I told you." Nora had phoned Jennifer the minute she hit the door, relaying the breathless details of her Orange Bowl encounter — well, *most* of the details.

"You didn't tell me *all* of it. You never *mentioned* the part about how you came up with the bright idea that the eighth grade should run the school." Jennifer leaned on one elbow, her black hair swirling down her arm.

Nora blushed. She hadn't told Jennifer quite everything about the Great Marc Johnson Incident. She glanced quickly at her reflection in the mirror over her dresser to see if her face was as red as it felt. How could she tell anybody, even Jennifer Mann, that while Marc was talking to her, all she was thinking about was being kissed by him? Jennifer would be shocked. After all, she — Nora — was the sensible one. Sensible people who wanted to be doctors didn't go around thinking about being kissed at the Orange Bowl.

"Well?" Jennifer prompted.

Nora regained her slipping composure. "Well — nothing. I forgot to tell you that part because . . . because it was so dumb. I didn't think Marc would even remember it, much less stand up in Mr. Robards' class and make a speech."

"Maybe he just likes to be the center of attention," Jennifer speculated.

"No, he doesn't," Nora responded, bristling. "I think it's great he cares what goes on at Cedar Groves as much as he does. After all, he just moved here. Marc Johnson is a sensitive, caring, *intelligent* guy. And those types are awfully hard to come by at Cedar Groves."

"Boy, you're really gone on him, aren't you?" Jennifer put her hand on Nora's forehead, as if taking her temperature.

Nora swatted her hand away, playfully, but she *was* annoyed. Jennifer didn't usually tease. Could it be Jen was jealous because Nora liked a guy and she didn't?

Surely a *boy* wouldn't shake the — so far — unshakable friendship. Would he?

As if sensing Nora's troubled thoughts, Jennifer said, "You know, I'm really proud of you for suggesting that our class could run the school. Nobody else came up with anything half that good. And Mr. Robards took it seriously! We might — we just *might* — get the chance to do it."

Nora flopped backward on her bed, as if overcome by the possibility. "Jennifer, can you *imagine*! All our lives our parents and teachers have harped at us for not being responsible. This is our chance to show them we *can* take care of ourselves."

"But running the whole *school* — " Jennifer bit her bottom lip, doubtful. "Do you think we can handle it?"

"Sure we can. But it's never going to happen. They'll vote us down at the staff meeting. Grown-ups never take kids seriously."

The next morning, Mr. Robards made an unexpected appearance in room 332, Mr. Mario's homeroom.

"I just wanted to let you know the result of yesterday's meeting," Mr. Robards said to the class. "If I have my facts straight, the 'Gripe Revolution,' as you so aptly call it, originated here, and I thought you people should be the first to know."

"Know *what?*" Mitch Pauley asked. He looked tense, awaiting Mr. Robards' pronouncement. Jennifer knew *she* was tense. She looked across the aisle at Nora. What had the staff decided?

Without further preamble, Mr. Robards said in ringing tones, "You're going to get your wish, eighth-graders! The staff has decided to let the eighth grade take over running the school — "

He was interrupted by a round of boisterous cheers. Tommy Ryder threw a sheaf of papers up in the air and Mitch Pauley pounded his desk. Jason Anthony did a war dance around his and Jennifer's desks, whooping like a maniac.

" — FOR ONE DAY," Mr. Robards yelled over the commotion. "And one day *only*. I think that's a fair compromise. Your teachers, yours truly included, would do almost anything to put an end to the 'Grumble Rumble,' as they call it."

"When?" Jason broke in. "When can we take over? Tomorrow? Do we get to pick who we want to be?" He stuck out his scrawny chest and pretended to puff a pipe. "I think *I* should be the one to oversee this whole operation. We need somebody capable."

"Which is why they won't pick you," Jennifer snapped. Would that boy ever quit getting on her nerves?

Mr. Robards was heading for the door. "I'll let Mr. Mario fill you in on the grisly details. I have to let the other homerooms know about the Big Switch. I'll see some of you later in class. We can talk more about it then."

Mr. Mario, who had been twiddling his pencil while Mr. Robards had been talking, got up and ambled to the front of the room.

If I get to run a homeroom, Nora thought, I'll certainly show a little more life than that man does. He ought to take vitamins.

"I hope you realize what a momentous occasion this is," Mr. Mario said, leaning against his desk as if he was too tired to stand up properly. "How many other schools would give in to the demands of a bunch of eighth-graders? It's certainly a first in the history of Cedar Groves Junior High. Of course, we want to do this right, in the safest manner possible, so if some of you" — he glared at Jason Anthony — "think that the staff and teachers are going to disappear for a day and let you all run amok, think again. This isn't going to be a free-for-all."

Denise Hendrix raised her hand and immediately every boy in class turned to stare at her. Jennifer wondered what it would be like to be that beautiful, to have boys gawking at you wherever you went.

"Yes, Denise?" Mr. Mario said.

"What are our parents going to say?" Denise asked.

"That's a good question," he acknowledged. "You'll find that out when your parents sign permission slips entitling you to participate in this — ah, experiment."

This statement was met with the usual groans that sounded whenever permission slips and parents were brought up.

"What if they don't sign?" Mitch Pauley wanted to know.

"Then you won't be allowed to participate," Mr. Mario said simply. "Mr. Robards has volunteered to head a committee that will iron out the details. Guidelines will be drawn up, *very specific guidelines,* to ensure that this program will operate smoothly and safely. We have chosen Monday as the day of the Big Switch."

"This coming Monday?" Nora asked.

He nodded. "The staff decided that the sooner we end this grumbling nonsense, the sooner we can get back to normal." Then he muttered, "Although after Monday, I wonder if we'll *ever* be back to normal."

The bell rang. Eighth-graders tumbled out into the halls, excited over the news. Nora grabbed Jennifer's arm as they headed for first period.

"Monday!" Nora shrieked. "It's going to happen! Jen, what did I *tell* you?" She laughed hysterically, still unable to believe that the teachers and staff had given in to the eighth grade! "Wait'll the seventh-graders find out. And the ninth-graders! They think they're so smart!"

"Thanks to you, Nora, we are going to get out of classes one whole day and take over the school!" Jennifer clapped her friend on the back.

"And thanks to Marc," Nora put in hastily, not wanting to hog the spotlight. "He was the one who actually suggested it to Mr. Robards."

"Yes, but it's still your idea," Jennifer insisted. She wished Nora could get through one conversation without bringing Marc Johnson into it.

Nora didn't notice the subtle shift in her best friend's mood. In her exhilaration she smacked a locker door, making a terrific racket, and cried, "Monday, the school! Tuesday, the world! Look out!"

The more Nora thought about it, the more she decided that the whole thing *was* her idea and it was a pretty good one. She kept reminding the others of that fact whenever the subject of the eighth grade running the school came up, which was about every two minutes. Why shouldn't credit be given where credit was due?

In history, Mr. Robards explained how

the Big Switch would take place. An agreement was drawn up, stipulating how the eighth-graders would take over the duties of each and every person who worked at Cedar Groves Junior High, from the principal right down to the custodial staff. There were approximately two hundred eighth-graders — more students than positions available. So the original "Gripe Revolution" homeroom had been chosen to participate, along with two other homerooms. The rest of the eighth grade would attend classes as usual, but lend their support in any way they could.

The teachers and the staff would attend school that day. But aside from emergency assistance, the regular staff would *not* offer any help. The eighth-graders were on their own.

Some of the jobs had been simplified. For example, the cafeteria staff would not be expected to prepare the usual variety of main dishes and food selections. Instead, the students filling in for the cafeteria workers would only prepare a single menu. In other positions, such as the custodial, nursing, and secretarial help, the regular staff would be on hand to explain certain particulars of that job, so the eighth-grade substitutes would know what they were supposed to do.

Nora thought the plan sounded rather

cut and dried. What had started out as a once-in-a-lifetime opportunity to show grown-ups that kids really *could* handle themselves was suddenly being weighted down with rules and restrictions. But then she saw the practicality of the plan. Not only would the eighth grade run the school and make learning *interesting* for the rest of the students, but they would do it within the boundaries of the rules set.

Nora's parents signed her permission sheet without hesitation. "I think it's a wonderful idea," Mrs. Ryan said. "You kids think everything is so easy. Now you'll get a little taste of what we go through every day." Mrs. Ryan worked as an attorney for Legal Aid. With two working parents, life in the Ryan household was sometimes hectic.

Without exception, parents of the selected eighth-grader participants signed the permission sheets, usually adding a note at the bottom that they agreed their child would benefit immeasurably from this experience.

On Friday morning in homeroom, Mr. Mario held up a bowl filled with little slips of folded paper.

"The lottery," he explained. "Each of you draws out one slip. On it will be written your fate for Monday. No trading. Whatever you take, you keep. Good luck."

Nora was shocked that Mr. Robards had chosen such a haphazard manner to delegate positions. She had expected him to assign duties according to each student's particular qualifications. How would deserving students rise to their proper stations by drawing papers out of a bowl?

Mitch Pauley drew first, then handed the bowl to Amy Williams behind him. He opened his slip, read it, and grinned. "All riiight! You guys are looking at the new boys PE teacher! On the floor! Fifty push-ups! Keep those arms straight!"

Well! Nora thought. He certainly got the right job. She watched the progress of the bowl up and down the aisles.

Denise Hendrix gasped when she opened hers.

Jennifer leaned over, concerned. "What is it?"

Denise's lovely face had gone as white as the paper she was holding. "I'm — the new school nurse," she said, her voice unsteady.

Immediately five boys doubled over as if they had acute appendicitis. "Help me, nurse!" one cried.

"You got the infirmary job?" Nora asked Denise. *She* had wanted that post! Wasn't *she* the one who wanted to be a doctor when she grew up! "That's a great job, Denise," she forced herself to say.

Denise covered her face with her hands. "For you, maybe. I hate it! I faint at the sight of a Band-Aid!"

Wonderful, Nora thought.

The bowl was getting closer. Steve Crowley drew the duty of seventh-grade geography teacher. Lucy Armanson laughed when she saw she was replacing her own math teacher, the one she had complained was so boring.

Susan Hillard wadded up her paper and threw it on the floor after reading her fate for Monday. "I will not do it! I will *not* be a janitor!"

Jason Anthony made scouring motions with his hands. "Let's get those toilets nice and clean, Susan!"

Then it was Jennifer's turn. Nora held her breath while her friend reached into the bowl and pulled out a slip. Jennifer unfolded the paper and read it, her face a mixture of emotions. She turned to Nora. "Guess who's the new assistant principal?"

"That's not so bad," Nora said generously. "You're sure to do a better job than Mrs. Peters."

Jennifer brightened. "You're right. Besides, I once heard that assistants are the ones who really run big corporations. The only thing is, they aren't filling her secretary's place."

By the time the bowl reached Nora there

were only a few slips left in the bottom. Nora dug around, then pulled out one. Her heart plunged to her toes with dismay when she opened her paper. On it was typed, "Cafeteria worker — Salads and Vegetables." Salads and Vegetables! Not even cafeteria manager! She started to throw her paper on the floor and declare the whole thing a waste of time, but then realized that it was all *her* idea. She couldn't act like a spoilsport now.

"What did you get?" Jennifer asked. "You look funny."

"You'd look funny too if you drew salads and vegetables," Nora replied. "Oh, well. I wonder if anybody in our homeroom will draw principal."

At that moment, Jason Anthony leaped up from his chair with a whoop. "Guess what, everybody! *I'm* the new principal!"

Nora couldn't believe it! Jason Anthony, principal! The biggest twerp in the western hemisphere drawing the most responsible job of all! Because of her, the eighth grade would take over the entire school come Monday morning, with Jason Anthony in the driver's seat, probably on his skateboard.

Even saddled with that handicap, she was sure running the school would be a cinch.

Chapter 4

"I'm scared," Jennifer confided to Nora on the bus.

Monday morning had arrived at last. Jennifer had nearly missed the bus, she had taken so long to get ready. She had changed her clothes three times, trying to find an outfit suitable for her first (and only) day on the job. After settling on a white blouse and a denim skirt, she tied a scarf into a neat businesslike bow around her collar, the way Nora's mother did. Now she smoothed her skirt, mostly to wipe the dampness off her palms.

"What are you scared of?" Nora asked. Jennifer thought her friend looked especially cool today, as if nothing could bother her. Nora was wearing white jeans, a white pullover, and white tennis shoes, the closest she could come to a cafeteria worker's uniform.

"Well, for one thing, I'm not the best

typist in the world," Jennifer said. "I know Jason will ask me to type *something.*"

"So? You'll do great. An assistant principal doesn't have to type. We'll *all* do great. You wait. They'll be so impressed, they might let us do this again, maybe one day a week." Nora was brimming over with self-confidence. Jennifer wished she could borrow a little.

"You seem so sure of yourself," she said. "You know, Nora, none of us has any *experience.* What if things go wrong?"

"What could go wrong? It'll be a normal day at Cedar Groves Junior High. The same classes and everything. The only difference is, the eighth grade will be running the show. Besides," Nora added emphatically, "some of us do have experience. Mitch Pauley will be perfect as a phys. ed. teacher. What better job for a jock? And I make the best tossed salad you ever tasted. Right?"

Jennifer nodded, but she was still skeptical. Over the weekend, she and Nora had gotten together at Nora's house to "practice" for Monday. It had all seemed so easy in Nora's kitchen. But the closer they got to Cedar Groves Junior High, the more nervous Jennifer became.

The bus pulled into the circular unloading zone. To the left of the buses a solitary figure stood beneath the rippling American flag. The figure saluted smartly as their bus stopped behind another bus.

"Who in the world is that?" Nora asked. "General Patton?"

Jennifer, who was sitting next to the window, pressed her face against the glass. "You're not going to believe this. *That* is Jason Anthony."

"Jason!" Nora exclaimed. "What on earth is he wearing? He looks like an undertaker." She crowded Jennifer at the window. "I didn't think they made black suits for kids that shrimpy."

Steve Crowley leaned over Nora and Jennifer to see the lone figure still saluting beneath the waving flag. "Good grief," he said when he realized who it was. "Shouldn't there be a band playing 'Hail to the Chief?' I think Anthony has let power go to his head."

Jennifer hoped not. It was bad enough she had to work in the same office with that creep. But to have to take orders from him would be the absolute *end*.

Denise Hendrix walked as slowly to the clinic as she possibly could. The halls were buzzing with seventh- and ninth-graders rushing to get to class before the first bell. Eighth-grade students she recognized hurried past her, their faces set in important expressions, their movements filled with purpose. Everybody seemed eager to get to their posts. Except Denise. If she could, she'd take the whole day to get to the nurse's office. She'd crawl on her hands and knees . . . she'd take the long way, via the Aleutian Islands . . . she'd —

She was there. The door was ajar and that horrible smell that reminded Denise of Bactine mixed with stale Cheerios and moldy bandages. Blood and guts — yuck! The smell nearly overwhelmed her. How would she ever survive an entire day?

A woman in a light blue uniform was sitting in a chair next to the white-blanketed cot, leafing through *Redbook*. When she saw Denise, she got up and said, "Hello. I'm Mrs. Haggerty. You must be my substitute."

"Yes, I'm — I'm Denise Hendrix." She looked around for another chair. There wasn't any. Her knees threatened to give way, so she sat down quickly on the bed.

"Oh, no, my dear," Nurse Haggerty cautioned. "You can't sit on the bed. That's for patients. Now get up and smooth out the wrinkles."

"But I — "

"Hurry up! You aren't on vacation, you know."

Denise swiped the wrinkles from the cover. Then Mrs. Haggerty showed her the contents of the first-aid chest. The gleaming wicked little scissors. The poisonous-looking bottles of iodine and other antiseptics. The rolls of adhesive tape and the packets of bandages. Tongue depressers. Jars of cotton balls and swabs.

"Will I have to use those?" Denise asked, her voice barely above a whisper.

The nurse shrugged. "Depends on what kind of emergencies you get today."

Denise swallowed. "Do you get many emergencies?"

"Some days are quiet," the nurse allowed. "But other days — " She rolled her eyes upward.

Denise stood helplessly next to the white table. She couldn't, positively *could not*, cope with any emergency. The mere *thought* of blood made her dizzy. Maybe if she told the nurse about her hospital-phobia, Mrs. Haggerty would sort of let Denise rest today, while she continued her regular duties. But Mrs. Haggerty went back to the chair and picked up her magazine.

Instead of reporting to the cafeteria first, Nora walked Jennifer to the office. "Your day will probably be a lot more interesting than mine," Nora reassured her. "You'll be where all the action is. I'll be behind the scenes tearing lettuce."

The door to the principal's private office swung open and Jason Anthony strode out. Nora muffled a giggle when she saw the tie he had on with his somber black suit — bright red with little green frogs all over it.

"You!" Jason lifted a stubby finger at Nora. "You're supposed to be in the kitchen. Get down there."

Nora was ready to fire a sharp retort but then remembered Jason *was* the principal today, which meant she was his subordinate, much as the notion galled her.

As she left, she heard Jason ask Jennifer if she took shorthand, he wanted to dictate a letter. Poor Jennifer! Maybe being assistant principal wouldn't be such a snap after all, not with Jason the Terrible breathing down her neck. Nora was almost glad she had picked the duty of cafeteria worker.

Nora paused at the doorway of the clinic to see how Denise Hendrix was doing. She was surprised there wasn't a line of boys waiting to get inside to have their pulses taken. Denise looked beautiful, if a little distracted, in a powder-blue skirt and sweater. She didn't see Nora, but stared hypnotized at the first-aid cabinet. Nora shook her head. Florence Nightingale, Denise was not. But at least things seemed to be going well in the clinic. That was what counted today.

On her way to the cafeteria, Nora passed Steve Crowley's seventh-grade class. Steve was sitting on his desk, swinging one leg and calmly calling the roll as if he taught geography every day of the week. He saw Nora at the door and gave her a thumb's up sign. Nora flashed the signal back. Yes, indeed, she thought as she strolled down the hall to the cafeteria, things were going very well.

She had barely put one toe in the kitchen when a voice barked at her, "Ryan! You're late!" Joan Wesley, an eighth-grader Nora knew slightly, came out of the cafeteria manager's office, carrying a clipboard. "Where have you been?"

"Well, I — "

"Never mind," Joan cut her off. "You lost your morning break. Now get an apron and a hairnet and get over to your station." Joan was normally a nice girl, but today the job of cafeteria manager had turned her into Genghis Khan.

Nora took a white apron hanging on a hook outside of the manager's office and tied it on. It was way too big; the hem flapped around her ankles. The hairnet was in an envelope in one pocket. She pulled it over her curls, glad she hadn't taken any pains with her hair that morning. She may not look so great, but health codes required food service workers to wear hairnets.

Nora had never been in the kitchen before and was amazed at the expanses of gleaming stainless steel, the enormous banks of ovens, and the huge dishwashing machine. She saw Mia Stevens on the other side of the room, her purple-streaked spiked hair mashed flat by her hairnet. Mia was arguing with Joan, gesturing wildly. Then Mia angrily took off her dangling earrings and scooped about two dozen bracelets from her arms, handing the jewelry to the manager.

"Over there, Ryan," Joan commanded, pointing to a stainless-steel table in the back against the wall. "Your partner is waiting for you. *If* you ever decide to get to work."

Nora looked to see who was going to help her make salads for today's lunch. Tracy Douglas was slouched against the table, her blonde hair tucked up in a hairnet, chewing gum. She blew an enormous pink bubble which splattered all over her face. Nora groaned inwardly. Some help!

In the span of two minutes, Jason Anthony had commanded Jennifer Mann to take a letter, get him a cup of hot chocolate, sharpen his pencils, lower the blinds in his office, water the plant, and send out for a bagel with cream cheese and extra chives. The new principal of Cedar Groves Junior High was drunk with power.

Jennifer had some idea of what an assistant principal's duties included and did not include. She stood firm against the hot chocolate, the blinds, the plants, and the bagel with cream cheese and extra chives. "I'm not your maid!" she told him indignantly.

Yet she felt a nudge of guilt over the shorthand. Was she expected to take Jason's dictation? She even asked Mrs. Peters, but the woman was like a brick wall, absolutely no help whatsoever. In fact, Mrs. Peters and Mr. Donovan, the principal, were holed up in an empty office, cackling over some joke with the guidance counselors.

"About that letter — " Jason began when she got back to her desk.

"Write it down," she snapped, "and I'll type it up. I don't take shorthand."

Jason gave her a withering glance. "The trouble with you assistants is that you're all too independent. If it weren't for me, you wouldn't even have a job." He sighed and audibly wished for the good old days when assistants did all those nice little things to make their bosses' lives so pleasant.

Jennifer didn't even hear him. She was too busy trying to figure out the typewriter. She plugged it in, turned on the switch, then panicked when the machine began humming impatiently, as if it wanted her to hurry up and get busy typing on it. Jennifer had never been so terrified of an inanimate object in her whole life. Where was the paper? She opened drawers and found some. How did she roll it in?

The phone on her desk shrilled. Jennifer picked it up and said "Hello" before she realized that was not the proper way to answer the school telephone. But the phone was still *ringing*, even though she held the receiver in her hand.

Jason came out of his office. "Aren't you going to answer that phone?"

"I would but I don't know how."

Jason punched a button at the bottom of the phone. "See that flashing light? That's the line that somebody's calling on, line one. What are you waiting for? *Say* something."

"H-hello. Cedar Groves Junior High." Jennifer covered the mouthpiece of the receiver and said to Jason, "It's some parent. They want to talk to the principal."

"I'll get him." Jason started to walk back to the office. "Wait a minute! *I'm* the principal. You don't cover up the phone that way. You put people on hold while you come tell me I have a call. Push that red button on the end."

Jennifer punched the red button. "Now what?"

"Now come tell me I have a call." He ducked into his office.

"You already *know* you have a call!" Jennifer argued. "Why make me come all the way in there?"

"Just do it!"

Jennifer stormed into the principal's office and yelled, "You have a call on line one!"

Jason punched the button and picked up the phone. "Hellllo," he said, his voice as oily as a late-night DJ's. Then he slammed the receiver down again. "They hung up."

The phone rang again. Angrily, Jennifer thought. She ran back to her desk, pushed the clear button, but forgot to punch the red button to put the caller on hold.

"You cut them off!" Jason sputtered. "If it rings again, I'll answer it myself!" The phone rang again. When he came out, his face was pale under his freckles. "That was a parent. Bus 270 never showed up today. A bunch of kids are still waiting at the bus stop, in the cold. It's almost nine o'clock. Where is that bus? How can we lose a whole bus?"

"How should I know?" Jennifer returned. "Are we in charge of buses?"

"We're in charge of *everything*!" Jason began yanking open drawers in Jennifer's desk. "Here it is."

"What?"

"The list of phone numbers Mr. Donovan told me about. Jennifer, you have to call the dispatcher at the county garage and ask him where the driver for bus 270 is."

Jennifer felt her throat tighten. "I can't. I hate making phone calls, Jason. Even at home. The only person I like calling is Nora and she — "

"We don't have time for this!" Jason slapped the list on her desk. The phone rang again. "That's another parent! They'll be calling all day to chew me out! We've got to find that bus! Now dial! I'll get that call."

He scurried into his office. Jennifer stared at the phone directory. There were dozens of names on the list. She had been telling the truth when she told Jason she hated to make phone calls. Phone-shy, Jeff called her. She couldn't even order a pizza without getting tongue-tied.

"Jennifer, are you calling the garage!" Jason screamed from his office, as the phone shrilled yet again.

"In a minute." Jennifer wished she could disconnect the ringing phone. How could she think with all that jingling?

"Not in a minute! Now! Right now! Get

to the dispatcher and *demand* to know where that driver is!"

With her finger, Jennifer marked the number of the county garage, but she was so nervous, her hand kept slipping off the list. Somehow she got the number dialed. The phone rang on the other end at least twenty times. Jason came out of his office.

"Did you get them yet? Hurry *up*, before another irate parent calls to bug me."

"I can't make them answer," Jennifer said irritably.

At last someone picked up on the other end. Thoroughly rattled, Jennifer forgot whatever manners her father had taught her and screeched, "This is Cedar Groves Junior High! Bus 270 hasn't showed up yet. Get that driver on the road immediately! What kind of sleazy operation are you running there, anyway?"

"Gimme that phone!" Jason grabbed the receiver away from her. His face blanched a shade whiter. He didn't say anything, just listened. The voice on the other end sounded like water on a hot griddle. Then Jason hung up. "Congratulations, Jennifer, you dialed the wrong number. You just bawled out the superintendent of schools!"

Jennifer pushed past Jason in her haste to get to the ladies' room.

Chapter 5

"Vasky."

"Present."

"Watson."

"Here."

Steve Crowley looked up from calling the roll of his geography class to see Nora Ryan standing in his doorway. She smiled proudly at him. He flashed her a thumbs-up, which she returned, then she left, presumably heading toward the cafeteria.

Yessiree, Steve thought. It's working out just fine. His seventh-graders were models of perfect behavior. They sat attentively at their desks, their hands folded before them, replying "Here" or "Present" as he called their names. Steve looked back at his class. They were so good. Maybe a little *too* good, considering he was their substitute. It was an unwritten law that kids always declared open season on substitute teachers.

He resumed the roll-call. "Zimmerman."

"Here."

It was time for the principal's daily announcements. Over the P.A. system came ominous cracklings, as someone in the main office turned on the mike. Then came a spitty-sounding *fooh, fooh,* as the microphone was tested. A high-pitched *skreee* nearly deafened them until the idiot managed to adjust the mike. There was a loud, amplified crash, then — nothing.

"So much for the announcements," Steve said, closing the roll book. His students sat up a little straighter and their eyes seemed to brighten. They were so eager to begin today's lesson! Well, he'd show them how interesting world geography could be.

Mrs. Strauch, the regular geography teacher, had left Steve a lesson plan. She had also asked him if he wanted her to stay in the room with him today. Steve politely refused both offers. He had glanced at the lesson plan and found it dull. *His* version of the building of the Panama Canal would be *entertaining* — the class would beg him to teach them more.

Teaching, Steve maintained, required the proper frame of mind, not just standing in front of the room relaying a bunch of dusty, dry old facts.

Something whizzed past Steve's ear as he reached for the textbook. A paper airplane. Steve spun around. "Who threw that?"

The class sat ramrod stiff, their hands clasped innocently on their desk tops. No one said a word.

A premonition, like the passing shadow of a winged monster, briefly pierced Steve's mind. If only one of them would *say* something. Steve decided the best policy was to ignore the incident. After all, these *were* seventh-graders. You couldn't expect them to act like grown-ups.

"Get out your books," he said, "and turn to page — "

Wham!

Thirty heavy geography textbooks hit the floor at the exact same instant. Steve nearly dropped his own book. Now that *had* to have been planned. Still no one in the class spoke a word. Not even a giggle. Their faces could have been carved from stone.

"All right," Steve said, tossing his own book back on the desk, as if relenting. "I agree. The book is dull. We won't bother with it today. Instead, why don't we have an informal class discussion. You know — just talk about whatever comes into your mind. As long as it's about the Panama Canal, ha, ha." He pointed to a boy in the first row. "What's your name?"

The boy never twitched an eyelash, much less answered.

"I asked you your name," Steve said, getting a little hot under the collar. "I *know* you can talk — you answered the roll."

The whole class responded by dropping their pencils in one perfectly choreographed motion.

They're doing this on purpose, Steve told himself. They wanted him to lose control. Well, he'd show them he wouldn't buckle under so easily.

He went to the board and carefully selected a piece of chalk, as if deliberating about what he wanted to write. Actually, he was stalling. He had no *idea* what to do next. His grand plans for making the Panama Canal entertaining had gone down in flames. Steve tried to think back to seventh grade — what did *he* like to do in geography that year? All he could remember was Christine Gregoire. She sat in front of him and she had long curly black hair. He used to take his pencil and gently, so she wouldn't feel it, slip his pencil through her sausage-like curls. He couldn't remember anything else about geography, just Christine Gregoire's hair.

He looked over his shoulder. His class was waiting, waiting, like a bunch of vultures. No one spoke. No one smiled. Did they all have lockjaw?

"Okay." He tossed the chalk back into

the tray. "I think what we ought to do is put on a little play. You know, act out the Panama Canal? They always say you learn by doing. So we'll rebuild the Panama Canal, figuratively speaking." He indicated the uncommunicative boy in the front seat. "You, you'll be Balboa. The rest of you in that row can be Spanish explorers." He went on to the next row. "You can be what's-his-name. Goethals, the engineer. And you next three can be the guys who signed the treaty. The rest of you can be engineers and diggers."

The class held their stubborn silence. Steve figured now they were quiet out of deep interest. Probably their teacher had never let them act out stories before. He came to the last row. Pointing to a girl in the first seat, he said, "You will be that health guy, Gorgas. And the rest of you — " He had run out of parts to assign. "The rest of you can be mosquitoes," he concluded in evident desperation.

"Okay." Steve was sweating. He hoped it didn't show. Never let them see you sweat, the commercial said. "Now, I want Balboa and you Spaniards to come up to the front of the room."

Nobody moved a muscle.

"To the front," Steve said, louder. "Come on, let's move it."

Balboa, the boy in the first row got out

of his seat. Instead of going to the front of the room as Steve had asked, he crossed over three rows and headed to the last chair in the back. The girl sitting in that chair went and sat in Balboa's seat. Before Steve could react to this novel display of mutiny, the entire class got up and switched seats.

"Real cute." Steve glared at his class. "Cut the funny stuff, okay? Balboa and the Spaniards, to the front."

This time the mass reshuffle took place without Balboa leading the way. The seventh-graders were in different seats again when everyone had finished shuffling.

"Okay!" he shouted. "I tried it your way! You don't want an interesting lesson today, fine, you'll get a dull one, just like you do every day. Get out your books and turn to page 223, and I don't want to see any monkey business. I mean it!"

Heads swiveled as everyone looked at everyone else. The stony faces broke into devious smirks. Steve shivered — his earlier premonition was back, in triplicate. He opened his mouth to speak, but whatever he was going to say was suddenly lost in a chorus of yells that nearly busted his eardrums.

Kids were everywhere at once — they swarmed over their desks like ants. A blizzard of spitballs flew through the air, followed by a hailstorm of erasers, papers, pens, and books. Two boys pitched the world globe back and forth. Steve wondered if he should call in the riot squad.

"I want order!" Steve cried, ducking as an unidentified projectile sailed over his head. "Order!" They ignored him. Frame of mind, Steve reminded himself. Teaching was merely a frame of mind. *Teach* those monsters! He couldn't even get them to sit down, let alone interested in the digging of some big ditch.

Steve ran to the board and scrawled "TRUCE!" between globs of spitballs, to no avail. Four more classes, he thought, crawling under the desk to avoid the flying objects. Four more geography classes to teach before he could go home and lock himself in a dark room.

Nora Ryan contemplated the fifty-pound sack of onions leaning against her work table. Fifty pounds. Fifty! She and Tracy Douglas had lugged the sack from the storeroom. The custodian in charge of the kitchen was supposed to do the heavy lifting, but Nora couldn't find him anywhere when it was time to bring out those onions. She didn't even know who he was.

"Fifty pounds," Nora said, awestruck.

Tracy popped her gum. "That's twenty-five pounds apiece," she said.

"I know that," Nora said sarcastically. Leave it to Tracy to state the obvious. "The point is, we have to peel and chop every single solitary one of those onions. And fast. We're behind schedule."

"How come we don't have a food processor?" Tracy asked. "We have one at home."

"Does this look like home? Even if we had a food processor, we'd still have to peel the onions by hand!" Honestly, Nora thought. That girl was so dense!

Joan Wesley materialized beside Nora, clipboard in hand. "Let's get busy on those onions, girls. Main Dish needs them."

Main Dish was Mia Stevens and another eighth-grade girl. They were making meat loaf, but it was the responsibility of Salads and Vegetables to provide the onions.

Nora stared at the schedule taped to the wall over her work table. The onions came first, then she and Tracy had to make coleslaw for six hundred. And then rice. And then go on the serving line. There weren't enough hours! How would they get all that done before lunch time?

She grabbed the mesh sack and ripped it open. Tracy just stood there, popping her gum. Nora handed her a knife, with a twinge of reservation, and said, "Grab some. We'll never get through if we don't hurry."

"I hate peeling onions," Tracy said.

"I'm not in love with the idea. But it's our job. Peel first, then we'll chop."

"Do we have to peel them *all?*" Tracy whined.

"We have to fill this pan." Nora indicated a stainless steel pan the approximate size and shape of a coffin. She grabbed an onion and began peeling. She finished that one and peeled three more while Tracy was still working on her first onion. "Tracy, you're going to have to move it!"

"I just want to do it right," Tracy said.

"We're not making onion sculptures! Just peel as fast as you can!" Nora looked at the sack. It looked as full as ever, maybe even fuller.

Then the tears started. Great big salty crocodile tears rolled down Nora's cheeks. After a while she couldn't even see, she had to peel onions by feel. Tracy was sobbing.

"I can't stand this, Nora! I have to stop!" she blubbered, tears streaming down her face.

"You stop and I'll kill you," Nora sobbed.

Tracy was on the floor, weakly paring an onion, and bawling like a baby.

"Get up," Nora ordered. "You can't peel onions on the floor. It's against the health laws."

Tracy struggled to her feet, then threw her apron over her face, as if she couldn't bear the sight of another onion.

Nora reached over and yanked her apron down. "You can't see like that."

"I can't see anyway!" Tracy wailed. "My eyes!"

"I know. Mine are killing me, too. Listen, let's talk. That'll take our minds off the pain."

"I don't want to talk," Tracy cried, miserable. "I just want to get out of here."

"Tell me about your new boyfriend," Nora coaxed. "What's his name?"

"I don't remember."

Tracy *was* in bad shape if she wouldn't talk about boys. "Okay, I'll talk," Nora said. "We'll soon be through with these onions — "

"Don't *say* that word!" Tracy squealed.

" — and then we can start on the coleslaw. That shouldn't be too hard. And the rice — maybe they let us use Minute Rice."

"Who cares?"

"*We* ought to care," Nora said. "For once the kids will have a decent lunch, because *we* cared. Nobody cares, that's why the food has been so vile. If the cafeteria workers were forced to eat the stuff they foist on us every day, then they'd make the lunches edible. Good nutrition is important."

"What good is good nutrition if we kill ourselves peeling onions?"

"Listen, Tracy." Nora couldn't really see her for the blinding tears, but she knew Tracy was there. She could hear her breathing. "The only reason we're here is because we are running the school. Have you forgotten? We — the eighth-grade class — are running Cedar Groves Junior High. We should be proud to peel all these onions."

"You don't really believe that baloney, do you?"

Actually, Nora wasn't sure what she believed. She had settled into a kind of stupor, brought on by onion fumes.

Reaching for another onion, Nora slipped on the papery onion skins that littered the floor around their feet. Who was going to clean up that mess? Where was that custodian?

Joan Wesley chose that moment to sweep past the Salads and Vegetables work station. "Hurry up, girls. You have exactly ten minutes to get those onions chopped." Then she noticed Nora and Tracy drowning in their own tears. "For Pete's sake, Ryan. Didn't you know you're supposed to peel onions under water?"

Nora resisted the urge to throw an onion at the back of Joan's head.

If I live through this, Nora vowed, I will never, *ever* eat another onion in any way, shape or form, as long as I live.

Chapter 6

Tommy Ryder propped his feet up on his new desk, laced his hands behind his head and leaned back in his plush chair. Guidance counselor had to be the cushiest, easiest job in the whole school. All he had to do was sit in Ms. Fauconnet's office and wait for students with problems to come to him for advice. Girl students, that is. Tommy was sure that once word was out that *he* was replacing Ms. Fauconnet, girls would be beating the door down to have a precious fifteen minutes of his time.

Tommy's office was between the extra, usually empty office at the end of the hall, where the principal and other staff members were whooping it up, and the area where Jennifer Mann and Jason Anthony were arguing. There was a loud crash from the principal's office. Apparently things in the front office were not going so smoothly. Another round of laughter erupted from the staff office. *Those* people were sure having a good time. Tommy wondered what they were laughing at.

A few minutes later, Jennifer Mann stomped into Tommy's office, startling him so he nearly tipped over backward.

He recovered quickly, as always. "Hi, gorgeous. Want to take a letter? On my knee, of course."

"Shut up. Just shut up." Jennifer tossed a pink slip on his desk and stamped out.

Whew! He'd never seen her so surly. That dumbo Jason Anthony was probably getting under her skin, Tommy thought, as he picked up the paper. The slip notified him of his first counseling appointment of the day. In ten minutes. A ninth-grader named Samantha Gardiner. Well, well! Things were looking up.

Tommy ran his fingers through his sandy brown hair, making sure it was touseled just a bit. He wanted to look like those guys on the front of *GQ* magazine, the ones with the slightly crooked ties and the horn-rimmed glasses. Intelligent but rumpled. He once read that older women really went for that kind of stuff. Too bad he didn't wear glasses. Tommy rummaged through Ms. Fauconnet's desk drawer. Aha! A pair of horn-rimmed reading glasses. He put them on. The room suddenly fuzzed over. Tommy took the glasses off and set them on the desk blotter in front of him, as if he had just laid them aside to think some really profound thought.

At exactly nine-twenty, Samantha Gardiner stood hesitantly in his doorway. She was as beautiful as her name, short dark hair, incredible gray eyes. This gorgeous creature had come to him for help, come to share her innermost confidences with *him.*

"Mr. Ryder," Samantha said. "Can I talk to you?"

"Sure. I mean — of course. Please sit down. What can I do for you today, Miss — uh — Ms. Gardiner?" Tommy wanted to laugh at the ridiculous formality of "Mr. Ryder" and "Ms. Gardiner" but then decided it was probably best to keep things on an impersonal level, at least at first.

Samantha plunked herself down in the chair in front of his desk, dropping her books and purse on the floor. "Oh, Mr. Ryder," she said in a teary voice that suddenly made Tommy very nervous. "I don't know where to start."

"Well — uh — why don't you start at the beginning?"

"Everything is ju-just terrible!"

To Tommy's horror, Samantha began to cry, loud, gulping sobs that shook the walls of his little office.

"Miss Gardiner — " he said with more

confidence than he felt. "You've got to get hold of yourself."

Samantha's yowls grew louder, if it was possible. The girl was definitely an unlovely sight now, with her red nose and crumpled face. She didn't even have a Kleenex. He saw a box of tissues on the bookcase. Tommy got up and handed the box to Samantha. She grabbed six or seven tissues and buried her face in them, but the sobs didn't diminish one iota.

Desperate, Tommy scanned the books on Ms. Fauconnet's shelf. Maybe he'd find some help here. He found a book called *How To Live Through Junior High School.* Samantha's sobs crescendoed. He could feel the reverberations right through his shoes!

The book was for grown-ups! Some kind of a guide to protect themselves against junior high school kids! What an insult!

He stuffed the book back in the bookcase. Samantha kept bawling, with no sign of letting up. Tommy wondered how she could cry that long without getting sick. He was feeling a little sick himself. Maybe he should go to the nurse's office and let Denise Hendrix take care of him. Yes, that was what he needed. A pretty girl to put a soothing hand on his forehead.

Denise Hendrix was in dire need of the cot, but it was currently being occupied by a ninth-grade boy who had checked into the clinic with a mysterious illness that seemed to travel from his stomach to his feet. Nurse Haggerty strongly suspected he was faking. Denise did too, but he asked to lie down and that was what the cot was for.

Denise couldn't care less about the boy's troubles, real or imagined. She was *dying*, positively dying.

So far that morning, Denise had been forced to handle three emergencies — three cut fingers, all boys. Of course, two of the cuts were *very* minor, not much deeper than a pin scratch. Still, Denise turned her head as she administered first aid, unable to look.

One of the boys called her an "Angel of Mercy," even after Denise had spilled a half a bottle of iodine on his pants. Denise knew she was no Angel of Mercy. She bungled everything she touched. Somehow the Band-Aid always wound up on *her* finger.

"Ooohhh." The boy on the cot emitted another moan. He did that every so often, just to let them know he had a legitimate excuse for being there. "Nuuuurse, could you come here a minute? I think I have a temperature."

Another boy lurched into the clinic, clutching his abdomen with his left hand.

When he saw the other boy lying on the cot, he said, "Get up, you! I'm sicker than you are!"

Mrs. Haggerty pulled a ball of knitting out of her tote bag. "Nurse Hendrix, you have another patient."

"I got a headache," said yet another boy as he staggered in. Behind him were at least four more boys.

"I'm sick."

"You got anything for bruises?"

"This kid hit me."

"Nurse Hendrix," Mrs. Haggerty said from her corner. "Your patients are piling up. You'd better tend to them."

The patients groaned and moaned, trying to get Denise's attention, but their complaints fell on deaf ears.

Jennifer Mann had just about had it with Jason. She knew she would never make it through the day without committing murder.

After the school bus mess had been straightened out, or covered over, to be more accurate, she told Jason it was time to make the daily announcements. She handed him the sheet with the latest basketball scores and after-school meetings of the various clubs. Recalling one of her contributions to the original Gripe List, she instructed him to read the announcements in a lively manner. Jason went into his office and closed the door.

Jennifer went back to figuring out how to roll paper in her typewriter when she heard the P.A. system click on, followed by Jason testing the microphone and then a loud crash.

She ran into Jason's office. He was sprawled on the floor, lying on his back.

"What happened?" she demanded, running over to him.

"I fell," Jason replied feebly.

"Off of *what*? How did you fall?"

"I don't know." Jason passed a shaking hand over his eyes. "I turned on the mike and then — I don't remember what happened next. When I woke up, I was on the floor."

Suspicion, like an ink stain, grew and spread within Jennifer. "How could you fall off a *chair*? Were you standing on it? I know you're short, but you're not *that* short. You can reach the desk without standing on the chair."

"I tell you, I don't *know* what happened. Instead of standing there gabbing, go get the nurse. Denise." Jason's voice went soft and gooey, like butterscotch sauce.

Jennifer knew then the little twerp was faking. She grabbed his arm and jerked him to his feet. "You're not hurt! You just want Denise fawning all over you! Well, it's not going to work, Jason. You're the principal, so start acting like one!"

She went back to her desk. Jason moped around for a little while, but when he strutted out of his office with a piece of yellow legal paper in his hand and a pompous grin on his face, Jennifer knew he was back to his old smart-alecky self.

"Type this up," he commanded, shoving the paper under Jennifer's nose. "And make me four copies."

"What is it?" Jennifer asked, trying to decipher Jason's unreadable handwriting.

"It's a speech I'm giving at the end of the day in a special assembly. Sort of a farewell address. Give people the chance to tell me what a great job I did today."

"Oh, brother! Does your ego know no limits?"

Jason flicked the carriage of Jennifer's typewriter. "Assistants are not supposed to make nasty comments. You can get fired that way. Don't forget, four copies, and you'll have to set up the assembly for, say, two-thirty."

Such a stupid speech! "*My fellow Cedar Grovians,*" Jason had written. Made them sound like some kind of aliens. "*We are gathered here on this grand ocassion to congratilate ourselves on a successful experment. . . .*" Jason couldn't spell any better than he could write speeches.

It took Jennifer forever to type that one page. When she was finished, she told her student aid to cover the phones, as she had to run off some copies.

The copying machine was down the little hall in the main office. Jennifer passed Tommy Ryder's office. The guidance counselor was trying to get Samantha Gardiner to stop crying, without any luck. Serves him right, Jennifer thought, remembering the way he had leered at Samantha earlier. He thought he was hot stuff. He didn't look so hot now. In fact, he looked like someone who had just had a large, heavy object dropped on his foot. Samantha was really getting to him. Jennifer had to admire the ninth-grade girl; she had never heard anybody cry so long and so convincingly. Jennifer didn't know why Samantha was pretending to have a breakdown in Tommy's office, but it was working. Tommy Ryder was visibly coming apart at the seams.

The copy machine was old and cranky. It wasn't like the copier in the public library. For one thing, there wasn't any coin slot. Also, there weren't any librarians conveniently around to help her run it.

Jennifer positioned the paper over the glass and closed the rubber lid. She pushed the "on" button. Right away the "add toner" light flashed.

Jennifer was stumped. She didn't even know what toner *was*. But it was a cinch that the copier wasn't going to work without it. She unlatched the front panel and studied the smeary diagram pasted to it. Toner was something that came in a bottle and had to be poured in a little hole somewhere. Sure enough, there was a box of white plastic bottles next to the carton of paper rolls. Jennifer unscrewed the cap and picked off the silver foil disk covering the opening of the bottle.

She studied the diagram again. The exact place she was to dump the toner was obscured by ink smudges. *Where* was she supposed to pour the stuff?

"Have you made my copies yet?" an imperious voice yelled down the hall.

Jennifer jumped, knocking over the opened bottle. "Jason! See what you made me do!" The clear greasy liquid was running all over the floor. "How am I going to clean this up?" she wailed.

"You don't," Jason said. "Call the custodian."

"You call!" Jennifer was nearly at her wits end. Her best shoes were getting all wet.

"You're the assistant!"

That's right, she was. Jennifer squelched back to her desk and rang the custodian's office. After what seemed an eternity,

Susan Hillard slammed into the main office, clanging her mop and pail.

"Susan!" Jennifer exclaimed, forgetting that she was one of the janitors.

"You were expecting Santa Claus?" Susan snapped. "Where's the mess?"

Jennifer pointed down the hall. Susan clanked by Jennifer's desk, glaring at her.

Susan Hillard was disagreeable most of the time, forever making sniping remarks. The pressures of cleaning floors and bathrooms had done little to improve her personality, Jennifer observed.

Suddenly Jennifer worried about the toll this day would take on the eighth-grade class. Running a school clearly involved more than high-flown ideas. It was mops and buckets, and crabby copier machines, and crying ninth-grade girls, and buses that didn't show up. It was *responsibility*. Assuming they actually made it through this day, would they still want to be friends with each other?

Chapter 7

The onions were done and now it was time to tackle the coleslaw. The cafeteria lady Nora was replacing for the day instructed Nora on what she had to do next. Nora wished the woman would stick around a little more, but the lady said she'd come back when Nora was ready to use the grating machine. One of the Big Switch rules required eighth-graders to be supervised by an adult when handling any potentially dangerous machinery.

"Seventh-grade lunch period is less than two hours away," Joan Wesley reminded Nora, as she slid by on one of her innumerable checking-up trips around the kitchen.

"I know! I know!" Nora turned to Tracy, who was draped uselessly over the table, picking a sliver of onion skin from under her fingernail. "Go over to Main Dish and get that dolly-thing away from Mia," she said. "We need it to mix the coleslaw in."

"I'm tired," Tracy whimpered. "Why don't *you* go get it?"

"You're going to be worse than tired if you don't do as I tell you!" Nora yelled. Why was it she was the only one in the entire kitchen who seemed to be taking her job seriously? Nora looked around. The bakers were standing by the ovens with quilted mitts, laughing over some joke. Mia and her assistant were wrestling with what looked like a lifetime supply of Gaines burgers, giggling hysterically when part of the crumbly mixture fell into the sink. Surely that gloppy-looking mess wasn't the main course for today's lunch?

Tracy came back, wheeling the enormous stainless-steel dolly-bowl. Nora had no idea what the contraption was, but Mrs. Lightfoot said they'd need it when they grated cabbage for the coleslaw.

The cabbage. The next item on the agenda. According to Mrs. Lightfoot, the cafeteria lady who normally worked in Salads and Vegetables, they would need two cases of cabbage and one case of carrots. Those cases were much too heavy for girls to lift. Supposedly a custodian was at their disposal for doing chores like bringing heavy food supplies from the pantry. But where was he? Nora hadn't seen any sign of him — she didn't even know who he *was.*

"Try the furnace room," Mrs. Lightfoot suggested. "Whoever is taking Mr. Mullens' place today ought to be there, since that's where Mr. Mullens usually is."

The furnace room was right off the kitchen, near the delivery entrance. Nora pushed open the door that said "Keep Out," angry because the custodian was sabotaging her already-too-tight schedule. A forest of pipes and joints and valves filled the spaces between the ceiling-high furnaces. He could be hiding anywhere!

And he was. Hiding. Nora caught a glimpse of a shadow and tracked it down. Lurking behind one of the hot water tanks was Marc Johnson.

"Marc!" Nora cried. "Are *you* the custodian?"

He yawned. "Yeah."

"What are you doing back here?"

"Nothing."

That was evident. "Don't you know you're on call in the kitchen? We *need* you up there."

"I've been busy down here, too."

"Really? What have you been doing?" Nora inquired, a knot of suspicion forming in her stomach.

"Things," Marc replied vaguely.

"Name one."

"Oh, this and that." His hand made a waving motion.

Marc took a penknife from his pocket and began scraping one of his fingernails. He was as bad as Tracy, Nora decided. No, worse. At least Tracy wasn't trying to hide. It was very hot in the furnace room. Marc's blond hair hung lankly over his forehead and his shirt stuck to him in spots.

"Marc, we've all got a lot of work to do. Who died and left you king?"

"What do you mean?"

"I mean, why aren't you pitching in?" He shrugged. "What's the *matter* with you?" Nora demanded. "You were the one who brought up this business of running the school in the first place. Show a little enthusiasm."

"It's hard to show enthusiasm for anything when it's ninety-five degrees." When he saw he wasn't drawing any sympathy, he sighed. "What do you want?"

"I need you to bring out two cases of cabbage for me."

Nora led the way, while Marc reluctantly followed. When he saw the cases of cabbage in the storeroom, he grumbled, "Those things must weigh a hundred pounds apiece! I can't lift those! I'll hurt my back."

"No, only forty pounds," Nora corrected. "If Tracy and I could drag out a fifty-pound sack of onions by ourselves, you ought to be able to manage those cases. Use the dolly if you have to." Honestly, Marc was such a wimp! It was one thing to be laid-back, but quite another to be just plain lazy. She was fast revising her opinion of him.

Complaining every step of the way about the splinters he probably got in his fingers lifting the heavy cases onto the cart and the fact that he probably sprained his back, Marc grudgingly hauled the vegetables to Nora's work station.

He started to walk away, leaving the crates piled on the cart.

"Wait a minute," Nora called him back. "You can't leave yet. You have to open the cases for me . . . and take them off the cart."

Marc Johnson was an utter, total disappointment.

But she had little time to think about Marc. Mrs. Lightfoot had set up the grating machine on the counter with the dolly-bowl positioned under it, so the shredded cabbage would fall into the bowl. She had also put the correct blade in the grating machine, since the girls weren't permitted to handle the sharp-edged disk.

"You just raise this lid, put the cabbages in one at a time, then push this lever," the woman instructed. "Couldn't be easier."

Actually, Nora could think of a lot of things that were easier. Carry-out food, for one. Why not just run down to the local deli and *buy* a bucket or two of coleslaw? But running the grating machine *was* a lot easier than peeling onions. Tracy handed Nora each head of cabbage and Nora fed the cabbage into the grater. Shredded, pungent cabbage fell neatly into the bowl.

Mia Stevens came over to chat. "The main dish is in the oven, finally," she said, leaning wearily against Nora's table. "If I never see meat loaf again, it'll be too soon. It was so yucky!" she lamented. "Mixing all those gross eggs and bread crumbs into the meat. I wanted to use a spoon, but the cafeteria lady made me use my fingers. Ick!"

"What are you complaining about?" Tracy said glumly. "We peeled all your dumb old onions for you."

"You were supposed to," Mia said. "That's your job."

"Maybe so, but it was a whole lot worse than cracking a few eggs." Tracy listlessly handed Nora the last head of cabbage from the first crate.

Mia widened her black-rimmed eyes. "A few eggs! Do you have any idea how many dozens of eggs I cracked?"

"It still wasn't as bad as peeling fifty pounds of onions," Tracy insisted.

Nora had heard enough. "Hey, you two. Let's not get into that — fighting over who's doing the most work. We're *all* working hard."

Mia sagged against the counter again. "I know. And I'm sick of it already. My feet are killing me. I'm so tired, I could just *die*. I want to go home."

"Go home!" Nora exclaimed. "You can't do that! Mia, this is our big chance to show the grown-ups we can handle what they do every day, only better. That's the whole *point* of all this."

"I don't care anymore," Mia said. "And I don't feel like I'm really contributing. I mean, who cares about us scullery girls back here in the kitchen? My idea of running a school is not making meat loaf for six hundred. And it's not just me. Ask the bakers. Or the dishwashers. They aren't so thrilled with their jobs, either."

Nora had to put the brakes on this kind of talk, right away. If the kids started complaining again, only this time over the work they had to do, things could deteriorate rapidly.

She traded places with Tracy. Away from the whir of the grater, Nora could talk to Mia better.

"Look, Mia, when we asked to run the school, that meant running *all* of it, not just the parts we liked. Everybody is important. Your *meat loaf* is important. If you made the best meat loaf in this school's history, then you should be proud."

Mia's expression got a little funny and she looked away. "I doubt my meat loaf will be the best in school history."

"What makes you say that?" Nora asked.

"Never mind." Mia went back to her own station.

Tracy shoved the last cabbage into the grater as Nora ripped open the cellophane bags of carrots. "I bet her meat loaf is just awful," Tracy declared. "She only makes C-minuses in home ec."

"We don't know that until we taste it," Nora said, still trying to keep an open mind, although it was getting harder by the minute. "Anyway, our coleslaw will be a winner."

"Do I put these in pointy end first?" Tracy asked, holding up a carrot. Nora pinched back a scream.

When the last of the carrots were grated, Mrs. Lightfoot came over to unhook the machine.

"What next?" Nora was almost afraid to look at the clock, suspecting she and Tracy were way behind schedule.

"Mix the dressing." The woman started to leave again.

"Where's the recipe?"

The woman half turned. "Oh, I don't use a recipe. I just mix a little of this, a dab of that. I've been doing it so many years, you see."

"But I *haven't*." Nora felt a wave of panic wash over her for the first time.

A few minutes later, Mrs. Lightfoot came back with a food-smeared looseleaf notebook. "It's in here, dearie, under dressings. And the measurements for the rice, too. Good luck!"

Nora flipped open the notebook.

She figured out loud. "For each serving line, we need about a gallon-and-a-half of dressing. We're having two serving lines today, so that means four of those great big pans of coleslaw, I think. If we double the recipe . . . oh, no, we don't have to," she corrected herself. "Looks like it's already been doubled."

Nora ordered Tracy to the pantry for three gallons of mayonnaise; a gallon of oil; salt, and sugar.

"What happened to Marc?" Tracy wanted to know. "Isn't he supposed to do the lifting?"

"Believe me, it'll be quicker if you do it. Hurry, Tracy, we haven't much time. We've got to get busy on the rice."

" 'Hurry, Tracy. Go to the storeroom and bring back a million-pound jar of mayonnaise while I sit here and read the recipe book,' " Tracy mimicked.

Nora put her hands on her hips. "Do you want *me* to go, is that it? I will, if I have to."

"Well, it's not fair. So far, *I've* done all the heavy stuff," Tracy whined.

"*You're* supposed to be my assistant," Nora pointed out. "All right! I'll go get the stuff. You figure out the measurements." Nora knew as soon as the words left her mouth she had made a fatal mistake. Tracy Douglas wasn't exactly Einstein in the math department.

But fair was fair, Nora thought as she wheeled the cart Marc had left standing in the middle of the floor back to the pantry.

"We need all that mayonnaise," Tracy announced when Nora brought the supplies back to their work station.

Tracy asked for the sugar canister. Nora winced. White sugar! Mayonnaise! Why not add hemlock and arsenic and be done with it?

Tracy dumped in four cups of sugar.

"Are you sure that's right?" Nora asked. "That seems like an awful lot of sugar."

"Read it for yourself."

"It says *two* cups of sugar," Nora said, exasperated.

"I thought you said we had to double the recipe. Two times two is four, right?"

"The recipe was *already* doubled. We needed *two* cups of sugar to make *four* pans of coleslaw. You put in twice that amount."

Tracy was amazingly unruffled, considering she had just ruined their whole batch of coleslaw. "Two lines. Four pans. Two cups. Who can get all that straight?"

"But, Tracy," Nora protested, ready to push her into the gloppy mayonnaise mixture. "You put in two cups too much. The dressing will taste horrible."

"I know. We'll just add more salt. It'll balance out."

Nora doubted it, but they didn't have any choice. The sugar was already mixed in the bowl. She never thought she'd live to see the day she had to follow one of Tracy's suggestions. Nora measured six tablespoons of salt, instead of the required three, hoping that would counteract the sweetness. With their spatulas, they started stirring the dressing into the grated cabbage.

With every pass of her spatula, Nora slopped the gooey white mixture over the sides of the bowl, no matter how carefully she stirred. Bits of mayonnaise-coated cabbage dribbled down the sides of the bowl.

"What's wrong here?" Nora asked, frowning. "Why can't we keep this stuff in the bowl?"

She didn't get an answer from Tracy, but then she didn't really expect one.

Nora glanced over at the stainless-steel pans on the counter. With a sinking stomach, she realized they had dumped the ingredients of the dressing helter-skelter into the same bowl with the grated cabbage and carrots. They were supposed to mix the dressing in those pans! No wonder the bowl was overflowing!

"Help me get this stuff in those pans. Quick!" By now coleslaw was all over the place — dripping down the sides of the dolly-bowl, oozing down the legs of the counter, and even on to the floor.

"What a mess!" Tracy remarked, as if it had nothing to do with her.

Nora grabbed one of the pans and used her spatula to scrape up excess cabbage. "Make sure nobody is looking!" she whispered to Tracy. They couldn't afford to waste any. Nora shoveled spilled coleslaw off the floor and into the bowl. She was usually a stickler for cleanliness, but this was an emergency. Besides, with all the cholesterol in that dressing, a little dirt certainly wouldn't hurt anybody.

Chapter 8

First and second period phys. ed. went like a breeze for Mitch Pauley. Of course, both of those classes were eighth-graders — kids from the "leftover" homerooms who weren't participating in the Big Switch. As most of those guys were Mitch's classmates, phys. ed. was more like their after-school games.

Mitch hummed a Springsteen song as he checked the schedule in the little office next to the locker room — he had ninth-grade basketball next. Good. Now he'd get the chance to show those big-shot ninth-graders a thing or two. He could hear the guys banging into the locker room now. They sure were loud — even noisier than the seventh-graders.

Mitch unlocked the equipment closet next to the gym. Twirling a basketball on one sure-fingered hand, Mitch glanced at the wire-covered gymnasium clock. Time to get those turkeys out to play ball. Mitch gave a mighty blast on the whistle he wore on a lanyard around his neck.

The ninth-graders did not come running out of the locker room as Mitch had expected. They marched out, slowly and deliberately, reminding Mitch of Roman gladiators entering the arena. The way they walked wasn't the only thing that made him think of gladiators. He gulped as his class surrounded him, like giant redwood trees circling a scrawny little bush. Mitch hadn't realized ninth-graders were so *big*. Man, those guys *towered* over him, made him look like — like Jason Anthony!

Mitch gaped at his class. These were no ordinary ninth-graders. No way they could have been from Cedar Groves — he would have *noticed* those big bruisers in the halls. Maybe they were seniors from the high school next door, who came in to crash the junior high gym. Or maybe — and this explanation seemed more likely to Mitch — maybe they weren't kids from this town at *all*. Maybe they had been imported from another school district, one where everybody hits six feet in grade school.

Whoever they were, they were waiting for Mitch to do something, waiting with expressions that made Mitch very uneasy.

"Okay," he said, his voice coming out in a mouse-like squeak. He cleared his throat and pitched his voice unnaturally deep. "You guys know what to do. Divide into teams, choose a captain, and get out on the floor."

He thought they'd laugh at him. Instead, they moved without any argument. Maybe this won't be so bad after all, Mitch thought with relief. When his overgrown ninth-graders divided themselves into teams on the basketball court, Mitch handed the ball to one of the captains, aware he had to reach *up* to give it to the guy. He blew his whistle again, mostly to have something to do, rather than demonstrating authority.

"Play ball!" he cried hoarsely.

His class began to play basketball, all right, but not the way Mitch had ever seen it played before. All two dozen players were out on the court at once, grabbing the ball away from each other. He gave a shrill blast on his whistle.

"Come on, you guys. Quit horsing around. Only five men on the court. You know that." He signaled the extra players to leave the court.

They ignored him. He might have been a fly on the wall, for all his whistle-blowing and hand-waving. They went on, playing their wild game of basketball, making up the rules as they went along. No passing, no dribbling. Not only did they "walk" with the ball, they also kicked it, rolled it like a bowling ball, and batted it like a badminton birdie.

Mitch blew on his whistle so hard, his eardrums hurt. "Okay! Enough! If you can't play right, maybe you'd better practice a few things. I want one line — around the gym and up on the bleachers. Ten laps. You hear me?"

If his class heard, they paid no attention. They went on, tossing the basketball over Mitch's head.

"Push-ups! Down on the floor! Let's go! Fifty push-ups. One, two — " Mitch's words bounced off the walls like the ball bouncing off the rim of the hoop. He began to wish he had drawn another teaching assignment — something real namby-pamby, like math.

Sometimes, when Lucy Armanson wasn't prepared for class, she hoped for a fire drill, especially in math, which wasn't exactly her favorite subject. But today was supposed to be different — Lucy was teaching her *own* math class. For once, she was prepared. But her class wasn't prepared to learn. Even more humiliating, Mr. Geiger, her regular teacher, was sitting in the back, observing his "substitute" in action.

Only there wasn't any action. It was

practically lunchtime and Lucy had yet to put the first equation on the board. Her third-period class was proving to be just as bad as the first two had been.

"Take out some paper," she began. "We're going to work the problems on page — "

"I don't have no paper," said a boy slumped in the front row.

"You don't have *any* paper," Lucy corrected.

"That's right. I ain't got any." This brought giggles from the girls sitting nearby.

"Why didn't you bring paper to class?" Lucy asked sharply, having been through this same little scenario twice before, in the last two classes. "You knew you had math today. Why didn't you come prepared?"

The boy shrugged.

Sighing, Lucy asked the girl across from him to lend the boy a sheet of paper.

"I don't have any paper, either," the girl said.

Lucy didn't know how to respond to that. She opened the top drawer of Mr. Geiger's — her — desk and took out a packet of notebook paper. "Anybody else need paper?" she asked.

The entire class raised their hands.

Lucy passed out the whole pack. When

each desk had one white sheet on it, Lucy continued the lesson. "Now, turn to page 171 and copy — "

"I don't have a book," said Randy Phillips from the other side of the room.

Lucy felt her blood pressure elevating to a dangerous level. "Somehow I'm not surprised, Randy," she said acidly. "You can share with the person next to you."

"She don't have her book, neither," Randy replied.

"She *doesn't* have her book, *either*!" Lucy said. What was the matter with him? With the whole class? "Share with somebody! I don't care who!"

"I forgot my book. Do you have yours?"

"Nope. I forgot mine, too."

"Teacher, I left my book in my boyfriend's locker and he's out sick today."

"I lost my book."

"My little sister flushed my book down the toilet."

Lucy had never heard so many flimsy excuses in her life. "Does *anybody* here have a math book?" she asked the class.

Randy pointed to the book she held in her hand. "*You* do."

"I can't give you this one!" Lucy said, exasperated.

"Why not?"

"Because — this is the *teacher's* edition. It has the answers in it!"

"Great!" said the boy in the first row. "That way we'll all get A's!"

Lucy went to the board and began copying the first equation. She'd show them that a little thing like not having any books wouldn't stump *her*.

"Psssst! Lucy!"

Lucy turned to see Andy Warwick in her doorway, motioning for her to come out. She stepped out of the room, a tactical error, she thought. Immediately a raucous cheer went up from her students, as if someone had just declared the day a legal holiday. She'd never get them calmed down now.

"Do you have any lima beans?" Andy asked.

"What?"

"Lima beans. I need them for my seventh-grade biology lab. They're supposed to dissect a lima bean as part of their assignment — "

Lucy still couldn't believe what she was hearing. "Lima beans? Dissecting lima beans?"

"Yeah. To study the little bitty lima bean plant curled up inside. You know, all that plant and seed stuff."

"Didn't you bring any lima beans?"

"A whole sack. But they *ate* them all. I don't know what I'm going to do with them now. You ought to see this class! If

I don't come up with something good, I might as well write out my last will and testament!" Andy did look a little worse for the wear. His dog collar was loosened and his hair stood up in natural spikes today, the kind you get when you keep pulling at your hair in aggravation.

"Sorry," Lucy told him. "I'm fresh out of lima beans."

"Too bad. Can you think of anything for me to have them do?" Andy really looked desperate.

Lucy shook her head. She was also fresh out of ideas and wondered how she was going to manage her own classes, much less have suggestions to offer Andy.

Back in the room, it took her fifteen minutes to get her class quiet again. When she felt it was safe to turn her back, she finished writing the problems on the board, then ordered her class to get busy working on the solutions.

"I don't have a pencil!"

"Me, neither!"

"Teacher, do you got a pencil I can borrow?"

"I dropped my last pencil down the sewer on my way to school."

Lucy squeezed her eyes shut and hoped — hard — for a fire drill.

If she never saw a can of Ajax again,

it would be too soon, Susan Hillard thought, dragging her cart of cleaning supplies down the hall. In her old life, back in the days when she was a normal eighth-grader at Cedar Groves Junior High, she often wondered why the janitors walked with such plodding steps. But now that Susan had joined the ranks of floor-scrubbers and window-washers, she *knew* why. Who would want to skip along to clean toilets? And how could she skip, even if she wanted to, weighed down with a ton of cleaning supplies?

Susan plodded down the hall.

So far her exciting day had included mopping up a river of spilled copier fluid in the office, fishing some seventh-grader's yucky retainer out of the drain in the girls' bathroom, sweeping up a huge pile of trash outside of Steve Crowley's geography room, unlocking fifteen stuck lockers, fourteen of which were jammed with chewing gum that you-know-who had to dig out, and pushing a broom down the long hall between the gym and the cafeteria.

And now, joy of joys, her next job was the unequaled thrill of cleaning all the girls' bathrooms. Susan plodded along even more dispiritedly.

It's lonely at the bottom, Susan thought. Nobody talked to her, not even the other janitors. The "custodial staff," a grand-sounding title that "galley slave" would more accurately describe, consisted of three members — Chuck Abernathy, who had luckily landed the role of head custodian, which meant he spent his time in the custodian's office ordering Susan around; Marc Johnson, who had disappeared into the furnace room right after the first bell and hadn't been seen or heard from since; and Susan, the only one doing any *work.*

Susan sighed as she pushed open the door of the girls' room. At that instant, the bell ending third period rang and there were suddenly twenty girls trampling Susan in their haste to get to the mirrors over the sinks.

The girls clustered around the mirrors, touching up their lip gloss and combing their hair. Nobody paid any attention at all to Susan. She might as well be invisible. At any rate, she couldn't get near the sinks until that giggling bunch left.

From her cart, she took a package of paper towels and unwrapped it. She started over to the dispenser near the door, intending to refill it. The bell rang again and the girls screamed as if they were late for being crowned Miss America, rushing for the door. For the second time in less than two minutes, Susan was stampeded by a gaggle of ninth-graders.

The sinks were clear, more or less. Susan caught a glimpse of her own face in the mirror. She looked gray, drab. She even looked *older*, as if three hours as janitor had aged her, made her haggard. Then she looked into the basins.

Susan wrinkled her nose. She was *not*, under any circumstances, touching those sinks with her very own hands. She wouldn't touch them even if she had protective gloves, which of course she didn't.

The sinks were definitely out. That left swabbing the floor and scrubbing the toilets. The toilets! Susan looked at the doors on the stalls hanging slightly open. There were five stalls. And this was her first bathroom. There were six more just like this one. Five times six made — thirty toilets!

She couldn't bear to *think* about it! Susan dropped her mop; the wooden handle clattered on the tiles. Her stomach swooped with a sickening lurch. She was sick, *sick*. Too sick to clean, that was for sure.

Susan left her cleaning cart where it was and ran up the hall, heading for the clinic. Halfway there, she realized that "Nurse Hendrix" was on duty.

Chapter 9

Jennifer felt like she was in kindergarten again, struggling with her backward N's. She was trying — and that was the word for it — to type a letter for Mr. Donovan, the real principal, to be sent to the PTA.

When her father and Jeff looked over the parental permission form, outlining the Big Switch, Jeff had said, "This will be a real experience for Jennifer. You know how they say a picture is worth a thousand words? Well," he added, his blue eyes sparkling, "Monday will be worth a thousand *years* of experience to those kids."

Now, as she rolled in yet another sheet of bond to begin Attempt #58, Jennifer glanced at the clock. Not lunchtime yet. Jeff had underestimated the years of experience by about a million. Jennifer wondered how Nora was doing. She probably had the cafeteria running like an operating room. Nora was a great organizer.

Jason's office door whammed open and he came bumbling out, wafting a piece of legal paper in her face.

Jennifer made a face. "Not another speech, I hope. The copier machine hasn't recovered from your last one. That's why it broke down, you know. It just couldn't stand duplicating that dumb speech you wrote."

"Very funny," Jason said icily. "And very out of line. Miss Mann, need I remind you that you are my assistant, not my conscience?"

"And need I remind you that there have been twenty-seven people in here wanting to see you about the ruckus in the boys' gym?" Jennifer shot back. "You refused to see any of them."

Jason plucked an imaginary speck of lint from the lapel of his black jacket. "I can't be bothered with trivial matters. I'm busy in there."

"Doing what?"

"Administrating. I am the principal of this school," Jason declared in a ringing tone that sounded like Patrick Henry demanding he be given liberty or death. Jennifer would have gladly given Jason either one.

"But Jason, you can't sit in your office and play ostrich. There's been trouble at the other end of the school. Don't you think you ought to go see about it?"

"Trouble? What trouble? I didn't hear about any trouble," he said loftily. "Besides, there's always a ruckus in the boys' gym — it's called PE. Nothing is wrong. How could anything be wrong? *I'm* the principal."

Jennifer drooped over her typewriter, pretending to gag. "Oh, brother!" With an egomaniac like Jason at the helm, their ship was bound to sink.

He handed her the paper. "Here. I want you to run this down to the kitchen immediately."

"What is it?" She peered at Jason's hen-scratchy handwriting. " 'Bacon burger, medium-well, French fries, onion rings, chocolate cake?' What on earth — ?"

"My lunch order," he finished. "Don't stare at me like that, Jennifer. You don't expect a busy man like me to eat what the *kids* are having, do you? Now, run along. It'll take those girls a while to bake the cake."

Before he ducked back into his office, humming, Jason straightened a plaque on the wall, one that didn't need straightening.

Jennifer was ready to toss his "lunch order" in the trash when she realized this would be a chance to go see Nora. She switched off her typewriter, glad of any opportunity to get away from the unfinished letter glaring at her. And Jason. What a *pain* he was!

She stepped out of the office, closing the heavy sound-proof door behind her, and into another world.

Chaos!

Everybody, it seemed, was in the halls. Bands of ninth-graders skulked around the lockers and whole platoons of seventh-graders careened up and down the halls.

Jennifer fought her way down the long corrider to the cafeteria, observing that the teachers-for-a-day were either not present in their classrooms, at least not where Jennifer could see them, or they were sitting uselessly at their desks while their students ran wild. All Jennifer could see as she passed Steve Crowley's geography class was a hurricane of paper airplanes. She could hear someone who *sounded* a little like Steve feebly calling the class to order.

As she neared the industrial arts end of the hall, Jennifer smelled smoke! She lunged for the alarm box next to a woodworking class when a fiendish cry caused her to look in. Unless she was seeing things, a group of seventh-graders were burning their hapless instructor at the stake! No, surely they were just burning a design into a piece of wood that was very close to the teacher. Still, the teacher wasn't moving, considering how close he was to the wood-burners.

Things were really out of control! And Jason was convinced everything was cool, simply because he was the principal!

Jennifer hurried around the corner, only to crash into Susan Hillard. Susan's face was the same shade as the cafeteria walls, a pale, pea-soup green.

"Susan! I'm sorry!" Jennifer exclaimed. "Are you all right?"

"Just fine!" Susan said sarcastically. "The thought of cleaning thirty toilets makes me feel so good, I'm going to the clinic to throw up!"

"I'm sorry you're not feeling well — "

"Not half as sorry as I am. Guess who has to take care of me? *Nurse Hendrix.* I'd probably be better off crawling in a hole somewhere to die!"

"Is it that bad?" Jennifer asked.

"Yes, it's that bad! In fact, I quit! Q-u-i-t, quit! I'm not touching a mop or a broom ever again!"

"Susan, you can't do that!" Jennifer said, horrified. "We're supposed to do our jobs for a whole day, no matter what. It's part of our agreement, the contract we made with the school staff."

"Well, I'm breaking mine. If anybody cares, they can sue me!"

Susan had apparently quit her duties some time ago, Jennifer thought, kicking a path through the ankle-deep trash that littered the hall. She had never seen the school look so messy and dirty. The place looked like a stadium after a big game. Had *all* the janitors quit, not just Susan?

The kitchen was as hot and steamy as the Amazon. And noisy! Workers yelled at each other over the racket of pans slamming against metal counters. Two girls rolled rattling carts of utensils to the steam tables set up behind the serving lines.

Jennifer looked around for Nora. She saw a girl from her French class sobbing over what appeared to be a pan of charcoal briquets. She saw Mia Stevens open one of the huge ovens and slide out a tray of something lumpy and reddish and very unappetizing-looking. The heat from the oven must have been terrific, because where hanks of Mia's dyed hair had straggled from her hairnet, there were purple streaks on Mia's forehead and cheeks.

At last she found Nora, sweaty-faced and short-tempered, rinsing out a ton of rice in the sink and arguing with Tracy Douglas. Whatever Nora was telling the other girl, it wasn't having any noticeable effect.

"Nora!" Jennifer cried.

Nora stopped spraying rice long enough to swipe a corner of her apron across her upper lip. "Hello," she said unenthusiastically, as if she barely recognized her best friend. "Did you come to help? As you can see, Tracy has slipped over the edge."

"Nora, I've had the most horrible morning," Jennifer said. "You can't imagine. First, there's Jason. He's getting on my nerves so bad, I know I'll never get through the day without murdering the little worm. I broke one copier and I think my typewriter is plotting revenge. And the phones! They never stop ringing!"

Nora wasn't listening. She was still fuming over yet another incident with Marc Johnson, the Harry Houdini of Cedar Groves Junior High. He had conveniently vanished again, just when Nora needed him to haul out sacks of rice. She and Tracy were hopelessly behind schedule. She was sure they'd never catch up. Actually, Tracy showed signs of never catching up and joining the *real world*, much less making a lunchtime deadline.

Disgusted, Nora had gone back to the furnace room. Sure enough, Marc was hiding behind a condenser unit, reading comic books. Comic books! Nora hit the roof.

"I can't believe you're sitting down here reading *Superman*, while the rest of us are slaving over a hot stove! What's the matter with you, anyway?" she raged.

"Nothing," Marc said calmly and went back to his comic book.

Nora ripped it out of his hands. "If you aren't in that storeroom in four seconds, I'm going to make you wish you *could* leap tall buildings in a single bound. Now, *move!*"

It was like pulling teeth. Marc went up to the storeroom, but only because Nora was right behind him, persuading him with the rolled-up *Superman* comic. He complained that the rice sacks were too high on the shelf, that he had to climb the stepladder to reach them and would probably hurt his back again.

"I suppose you want me to haul this stuff all the way into the kitchen." Marc grudgingly loaded the rice onto the cart.

"No, I want you to take the rice outside and pour it down the storm drain. Of *course* I want it in the kitchen! Where else?" Nora followed him to make sure he didn't grab a catnap on the way. "Do you think it would be too much trouble to open the sacks?" she asked between gritted teeth.

"I'm on my break," Marc whined.

"If you don't tear those sacks open, you'll be on a permanent break," Nora threatened. *What* did she ever see in that guy? How could she ever have believed, even for an *instant*, that Marc Johnson was so perfect? He wasn't all that handsome, either. The corners of his mouth turned down, making him look like a sour old man.

But the straw that broke the camel's back was Tracy. She simply checked out, leaving no forwarding address. Nora couldn't get her to help dump the rice in the sink so they could rinse it. She wouldn't do *anything* now, except wipe that same stupid spot on the counter. How would Nora ever manage on her own? Though Tracy wasn't very useful, she was *some* help. Nora took a swift glance around the kitchen.

"Jennifer," Nora said now. "I didn't see you standing there."

"Nora! I've been talking to you for five whole minutes! Haven't you heard a word I've said?"

"Oh, sure," Nora replied absently. "I'm just so busy. I really don't have time for chit-chat, Jen. I've got to get this rice in the oven, if the school is going to eat on time. *White* rice," she added, more to herself than to Jennifer. "Not even brown rice."

"Why doesn't Tracy help you?" Jen asked.

Nora swished the sprayer one last time over the sinkful of soggy rice. "Tracy is in the twilight zone."

"I am not," Tracy said, speaking for the first time in more than half an hour. "I've been thinking."

"Again? That makes twice this year." Nora wasn't usually so sarcastic to Tracy, not the way Susan Hillard always was, but today she was too harried to spare people's feelings.

"What have you been thinking about?" Jennifer asked her.

Tracy stopped rubbing the spot on the counter and looked at Jennifer with wide blue eyes. "I've decided I'm not going to be a cook when I grow up."

"Five million stomachs in America thank you," Nora mumbled. "Tracy, since you've come back to life again, why don't you help me get this rice into the pans?"

"All right. But you have to tell me how to do it. Do we use a spatula?" Tracy asked.

"Too slow. Just use your hands, if you remember how."

A resounding crash made Jennifer jump.

"That's only Marcie," Nora said. "One of the bakers. Smell that delicious aroma? Parker House rolls, burned to a cinder."

"Nora," Jennifer said, trying to get her friend's attention. "What are we going to do? You ought to see the mess in the halls. Kids are running around, the teachers are in hiding — "

"—along with one janitor," Nora put in.

"Jason thinks things are just fine. I tried to tell him the school is falling apart, but he won't listen."

"Yes, well, we all have our problems," Nora said, tipping out a gallon of wet rice with her hands and dumping it into a pan the size of a bathtub.

"He's so out of it, he even sent me down here with a special lunch order," Jennifer went on.

Nora stopped to stare at her friend. "What did you say?"

Jennifer pulled the paper from her pocket. "This is what Jason wants for lunch. A bacon burger, medium-well, French fries, onion rings, and choco—"

"Is he crazy!" Nora shrieked, startling Tracy who dropped her handful of rice on the floor.

Nora snatched the paper from Jennifer with rice-coated fingers. "Chocolate cake! Onion rings!" She crumpled up the paper and threw it on the floor. "You tell that meathead he's getting meat loaf like everybody else! This isn't the Waldorf-Astoria!"

Nora and Jennifer exchanged a look that clearly said: *If we get out of this alive, we will never complain about anything ever again.*

Chapter 10

The clinic was packed to the rafters with patients. Denise did not have room to turn around, much less treat all those people. The ninth-grade boy with the mysterious traveling pains was forced to give up the luxury of lying on the cot. Now he sat up on the edge of the bed, along with five other boys. Other patients were sandwiched between the table and the door. Susan Hillard was gazing sightlessly at a chart depicting the Heimlich Maneuver. "I knew it," she kept saying. "I knew this place would be insane."

From her corner, Mrs. Haggerty said to Denise, "I think some of these people can go back to their classes, after you check them over and discharge them. They don't look very sick to me. Of course," she added, her knitting needles flying, "I can't tell you how to run your infirmary, Miss Hendrix. That's for you to decide."

The last thing Denise wanted to do was examine a roomful of moaning, groaning people, faking or not. Suppose they *weren't* faking? How was she to know?

Denise couldn't think with so many bodies crowding the tiny room. "We need more chairs," she said, at last coming to some sort of decision.

Immediately two of the boys on the cot leaped to their feet, chorusing, "I'll get them!"

Three boys hovering near the doorway fought to do the honor.

"No, let me!"

"I'll be glad to get some chairs, Denise!"

"How about a loveseat?"

"Shut up, fathead!"

Denise pushed through the mob. "I'll get them myself." She called back to Mrs. Haggerty, "I'm going up to the office."

And out the front door if anybody tempts me with a ride home, she thought, drawing deep lungfuls of nonantiseptic-smelling air. If felt so good to get out of that horrible place, Denise almost skipped to the office.

There were an awful lot of kids milling around, Denise noted, stepping around a group of seventh-grade girls who were sitting on the floor with a copy of *Seventeen* magazine between them. They were chewing on long whips of cherry licorice, as casually as if they were lolling around the park, completely unconcerned that they were skipping class.

"Did the bell ring?" Denise asked one of the girls. "I didn't hear it." That had to be the only logical explanation for so many kids to be roaming the halls.

"Did you hear the bell?" the girl echoed to her friend.

"Sure. It went *ding-dong, ding-dong!*" The girls cracked up.

"That's not all that went ding-dong," Denise said. She should have known better than to ask a seventh-grader anything. After all, they were still babies of *twelve*, while Denise was going on fifteen. Most of the time Denise was not bothered by the fact that she was older than most of the others in her class. It wasn't her fault she was older than most of the kids in the eighth grade — blame it on her European education and all the moving around she did when she was younger. But sometimes, like now, she felt a *lot* older than the other kids.

As Denise picked her way up the hall, she thought about the Big Switch. Surely the other eighth-graders were doing a better job than *she* was today, despite her advanced age and European education. If she only hadn't gotten the job of nurse. . . . In *any* other post, her level of maturity would have allowed her to shine, to be a real asset to the school.

Inside the office, she found Jason Anthony and Jennifer Mann at the long counter, wrestling over the microphone used to make PA announcements. Jason's level of maturity, if he'd ever had one, seemed to have plummeted below sea level.

Joan Wesley was there, too, waving her clipboard. "Listen, you guys, you'd better make *some* kind of an announcement soon, before the next bell. If those seventh-graders are let loose in the cafeteria, thinking lunch is going to be served on time, we're in for it. They already know that just for today lunch will be served in shifts. Now we have to tell them it will be late."

"Exactly how much are you running behind?" Jennifer asked Joan.

Joan consulted her clipboard, as if searching for the answer there. "See, we had to bake more rolls. The bakers burned all eight pans and I sent one of the girls to the clinic to lie down, she was so hysterical."

Wonderful, Denise thought. Just what I need.

"I pulled one of the dishwashers off to help the other baker," Joan went on.

Jennifer looked confused. "Are you going to be able to serve lunch at all today?"

"Oh, yeah," Joan reassured her. "We're just a few minutes late, that's all. That's why I need you to make an announcement."

"Exactly how much time are you running behind?" Jennifer repeated, her voice even. Denise was impressed — Jennifer seemed very composed.

"About twenty minutes," Joan said. "We should be able to start serving at eleven-forty-five."

Jason surrendered the microphone and began scribbling furiously on a piece of paper. "If we cut fourth period short and move fifth period up — "

Jennifer snatched the paper away from him. "We don't need to move fifth period anywhere! We're only delaying lunch twenty minutes, didn't you hear Joan? We'll just extend fourth."

"Listen, Jennifer," Jason warned. "I'm in charge of any schedule changes around here, not you."

"I'll leave you guys to fight it out," Joan said, heading for the door. "I've got to get back to the kitchen and make sure it's still in one piece. Do something quick, before the next bell."

Jason turned on the microphone and blew into it to make sure it was working. "Attention, all faculty and students, attention," he said in a voice like a foghorn.

"This is your principal. We interrupt your classes for this special bulletin — "

Jennifer punched him. "Will you get *on* with it?"

" — I regret to inform you that, due to circumstances beyond our immediate control, seventh-grade lunch period will be postponed, and so will eighth-grade lunch period, and — uh — ninth-grade lunch period. Subsequently, fifth and six periods will be shifted to accommodate — "

Jennifer grabbed the microphone, pushed Jason to one side, and said clearly, "Seventh grade lunch period will begin today at eleven-forty-five, instead of eleven-twenty-five. Stay in your fourth-period rooms until the bell. All other lunch periods will also be delayed twenty minutes. We are sorry for the inconvenience." She shut the microphone off before Jason could do any further damage.

"I was *going* to tell them," Jason said petulantly. "You didn't have to shove like that."

"Jason, you were giving them such a load of gobbledygook, they'd never figure it out." Then Jennifer noticed Denise standing there. "Oh, hi, Denise. Can I help you?"

"I hope so," Denise said.

Jason scampered around the counter. "Denise! Is this a house call? Were you worried about me in this highly stressful position? I do have a splitting headache. Maybe you and me could go in my office and you could — ”

Jennifer cut him off. “Denise already knows how sick you are, Jason. Mentally, that is. Denise, did you want something?”

“It’s standing-room-only in the clinic. Can I borrow some chairs?”

“Chairs!” Jason cried eagerly, as if he’d just struck oil. “I’ll get them! You shouldn’t be lifting heavy furniture, Denise. That’s a job for a man.”

“Do you know where we can find one?” Jennifer asked sarcastically. “Jason, that’s *my* chair! Put it back!” She rolled her eyes at Denise. “Can you believe that idiot? He’ll probably come back with *his* chair.”

He did. Jennifer made him put the principal’s leather swivel chair back in his office. Finally, Jennifer directed him to take three visitors’ chairs to the clinic. She and Denise watched him stagger down the hall with all three chairs.

“How’s it going?” Jennifer asked her.

Denise stared at the floor. “Not good. I hate it in the clinic.”

Jennifer patted her shoulder. “I know. It’s no picnic here in the office. But look at it this way, Denise. The day is half over, almost. You can stand anything for a few more hours.”

Denise wasn't so sure of that.

Nora's morning had disintegrated from bad to awful. If the temperature in the kitchen rose another tenth of a degree, she knew she'd keel over with heatstroke. Plus, everybody kept running to her with their troubles. As if Nora didn't have enough troubles of her own to contend with.

First it was the bakers. Both girls ran over to Nora, sobbing because they had burned every single pan of Parker House rolls. Nora spared them little sympathy.

"What're we going to *do*?" one of the girls bawled.

"Bake some more," Nora told her, heartlessly.

This was too much for the other girl. She started wailing. Joan Wesley sent her to the clinic and assigned one of the dishwashers to take her place.

Then Mia Stevens came over to Nora's station. She was crying, too. "My meat loaf," she sniveled. "It won't slice."

"What do you mean, it won't slice? Did you let it cool?"

Mia nodded, her mascara leaving charcoal-colored tracks down her cheeks. "It just falls apart. I can't slice it. They're going to have to eat it with a spoon!"

"Who ever heard of meat loaf you have to eat with a spoon?" Nora said scornfully.

"Meat loaf by definition is something that you slice and eat with a *fork.*"

"Not my meat loaf," Mia said. "It's too runny."

Nora elbowed her out of the way. "Gee, that's too bad, Mia. I'd like to help, but I've got work of my own to do. Tracy!"

Tracy had drifted away again, this time chatting with the other dishwasher. Nora considered tying her to the table.

"Tracy, get over here!"

Tracy sulked back over to Salads and Vegetables. "What do you want now?"

"In case you have forgotten, we still have to make the rice."

Mrs. Lightfoot had informed Nora that they'd need eight pans of rice, but the recipe book only gave measurements in gallons and pounds, not pans. A pound of rice to a gallon and a half of water. How many pans did that make? Nora looked at the two twenty-five pound sacks of rice Marc had deposited on the floor. How many pounds went into a gallon?

"Okay," she told Tracy. "We'll put about four inches of rice in the pans and then add the butter and water. Where are you going?"

"To the office."

"What *for*?" Nora's voice was raw with exasperation.

"A ruler. To measure the rice with."

"We don't need a ruler. Just *guess* four inches. Can you do that?" Nora set a pan on the floor, then tipped the sack until she had poured enough rice in it. Tracy did the same with her sack until all eight pans were full and both sacks were empty.

"That looks like an awful lot of rice," Tracy remarked. "Do you think we used too much? We only made six pans of coleslaw."

"Mrs. Lightfoot said we'd need more rice. It's fluffier, not dense like the coleslaw." Nora carelessly dumped a whole pound of butter in each pan without even flinching at the amount of cholesterol. The butter was supposed to be chunked, not left in a big lump, but there just wasn't time. The heat from the oven would melt the butter anyway. With the spray attachment on the faucet, Nora added water to the top of the pans. Then she and Tracy covered the pans with heavy-duty aluminium foil and hefted the first pan onto the cart.

"Ooompf!" Tracy let her end go too soon and water sloshed out from under the aluminum foil. "Gosh, these are heavy!"

"Stop dawdling, Tracy! We've got to get these pans in the oven." They loaded the other pans on the cart and wheeled the cart over to the bank of double ovens.

The bakers were sliding pans of fresh Parker House rolls into the more convenient, lower row of ovens. The rolls looked like they were made of Play-Doh, Nora observed.

"Move your stuff into the top ovens," Nora said immediately. "We need the bottom ones."

"We were here first," the dishwasher-promoted-to-baker said in a snide tone.

"Don't be stupid," Nora said. "We can't possibly lift these heavy rice pans over our heads. Now get those rolls out of my way." She spoke with such brisk authority, the other girls hastened to move their pans into the top ovens.

While the rice was baking, Nora had Tracy clean up their station, while she gathered up leftover supplies to return to the pantry. In the huge, walk-in pantry, Nora found Marc Johnson eating a salami sandwich. He grinned guiltily.

"Caught in the act," he said, taking a big bite.

Nora was so hungry that even nitrate-loaded salami looked good to her. It seemed like *days* since she had eaten breakfast. "Where did you get that?" she demanded.

He pointed to the gigantic roll of salami hanging from a hook and the opened package of bread. "Right there. Mr. Mullens said it was a privilege of the job. He raids the pantry all the time."

"Maybe he earns the right, but you certainly haven't," Nora snapped. "I think you better take that sandwich back to your nest behind the furnace before I do something violent."

"Boy, what a grouch!" Marc said.

"You'd be grouchy, too, if you'd worked as hard as I have this morning."

"Hey, man," he said in that cool California drawl that no longer thrilled her. "I've done my part."

"You haven't done *anything*, except by force," Nora argued. How could someone who had given such a fiery, convincing speech about democracy and letting the eighth-graders have their chance turn into such a shiftless slug?

"You know," he said, polishing off his sandwich. "I used to think you were okay, but now — " He shook his head.

He left, split seconds before Nora could club him with the salami.

Tracy's attempts to clean up were pathetic at best. Nora grabbed the sponge away from her and wiped up most of the mess herself.

"It's time to check the rice," Nora told Tracy.

"You check."

"We'll *both* check." She dragged Tracy over by her apron strings. Nora put on quilted oven mitts and opened two of the oven doors at once. Rice boiled over the pans and flowed like lava down the front of the oven. *Tons* of rice.

Nora screamed. "Tracy — !"

But Tracy had already opened the other two ovens. A thick curtain of rice bubbled over the lip of the oven doors and spilled down the side to the floor.

"Quick! Get a pan! A lot of pans! Bowls!" Nora cried hysterically. She began grabbing pans, pot lids, collanders, anything that would hold the rice that was still pouring out of the ovens like soap suds.

Mia Stevens ran over with the dolly-bowl on wheels and helped Nora and Tracy shovel the foaming rice into containers before it hit the floor.

When it was over, Nora was exhausted. They had managed to save about half of the rice. She hoped they wouldn't run short on the serving line. Joan Wesley came out of her office then, ordering the servers to take their places on the line.

Nora trudged to the steam tables. Her work was far from over — the worst, in her opinion, was yet to come. She had to serve meat loaf that wouldn't slice, coleslaw that was too sweet, rolls that were burned on the outside and doughy in the middle, and rice that had been tossed around like popcorn.

Chapter 11

Jennifer stood on tiptoe outside the boys' gym and peered through the high, wire-screened window in the metal door. Through the glass she saw a blur of basketballs, baseball gloves, hockey sticks, volleyballs, tennis shoes — all flying through the air as if caught up in a whirlwind. Good thing she came down here to see for herself. Jason certainly wasn't about to take any action, even after a bunch of terror-stricken seventh-grade boys burst into the office to report that a band of renegade ninth-graders had taken over the boys' gym and wouldn't let them in. Jason ignored their story, but Jennifer could see with her own eyes that it was true.

Clearly something had to be done, but what? Jennifer wasn't much good at putting down riots. She leaned against the crash bar to think over the situation. What

would Nora do in her place? Nora wasn't afraid of anything, hardly.

Clunk! The force of a solid, massive object, possibly a body, slammed into the door, jolting Jennifer out of her thoughts. Things were really getting rough in there! Where was Mitch? Were the rowdy ninth-graders holding him hostage in the locker room?

Without hesitation, Jennifer pushed on the crash bar and stormed the boys' gym.

No one noticed her spectacular arrival, but that was hardly surprising. The noise was terrific! Boys howled and shouted as they threw anything that wasn't bolted to the floor. And they were so big! Jennifer couldn't recall seeing those boys around Cedar Groves — they must be from another school. No wonder it was total anarchy in here. They didn't even belong in Cedar Groves!

In the middle of the confusion a lone figure tottered on the foul line of the basketball court, blowing a whistle in feeble, reedy-sounding little *whees*. Mitch Pauley. He looked shell-shocked, dazed, as if he had stumbled into the middle of a fireworks display.

Jennifer couldn't think of anything else to do, but she knew she had to get him out of there, to some place safe. Before she could make a move in his direction, an enormous ball hurtled across the gym, heading right for Mitch!

"Mitch!" Jennifer shrieked.

He turned at the sound of her voice, but it was too late. The medicine ball bonked him square on the forehead and he pitched over like a tenpin. The heavy, stuffed leather ball dropped nearby like an unexploded bomb.

Jennifer ran to Mitch and knelt at his side. "Mitch! Are you okay?"

Mitch groaned and rolled over, but he didn't speak.

Jennifer pulled him back so she could look at his head. There was a dilly of a lump blooming in the middle of his forehead that could have been either from the medicine ball or his fall. He opened his eyes and gazed up at her blankly.

"Mitch, can you hear me?" Jennifer shook him gently.

For an answer, he merely groaned again.

Jennifer shot to her feet and grabbed the nearest boy by a fistful of T-shirt. "Stop that carrying on! Right now! Can't you see you've hurt somebody?"

The boy stared owl-eyed at Jennifer. She was uncomfortably aware that he was at least six inches taller than she was.

"Help him up," she commanded the flabbergasted ninth-grader before her courage deserted her entirely. "Do you hear

me? He's hurt — he has to go to the clinic."
She took one of Mitch's arms; the other boy did the same. Together, they got Mitch to his feet. Mitch's legs wobbled like they were made of Jell-O and his head lolled on Jennifer's shoulder. She was really worried. A head injury was nothing to mess around with.

"Let us through!" she snarled as she and the ninth-grade boy half carried, half dragged Mitch across the gym floor. Astonishingly, the yelling and throwing paused as the revelers parted to let them pass. One boy even opened the door for them.

At the infirmary, there were people — all boys, Jennifer noted — hanging out in the doorway. "Get out of the way!"

Jennifer and the ninth-grader pulled Mitch into the room. "Where's Denise? Denise, are you in here?" Jennifer had never seen so many boys crammed into one place in her entire life.

She saw Susan Hillard backed up against the wall. "What's going on?" Jennifer asked her. "Is there an epidemic?"

"Yes, an epidemic of Denise Hendrix admirers," Susan said wryly. "Isn't it disgusting? What's wrong with Mitch? He doesn't look like he's faking, unlike the rest of these bozos."

"He isn't. He got hit on the head with a

medicine ball." She finally spied Denise. "Denise, we need some help — can you clear those guys off the cot?"

Denise looked almost as befuddled as Mitch. She didn't respond for about a minute. Jennifer couldn't stand there holding Mitch up all day — she barked out an order and five boys moved off the cot instantly. When Mitch was stretched out on the cot, groaning that his head was killing him, Jennifer turned to Denise.

"I've got to get back to the office and tell Jason there's been an accident. Can you take care of him?"

Denise didn't reply.

"Denise . . ." Mitch said faintly.

"He can't be too bad off," Susan remarked. "He's just like all the other boys in here, wanting Denise's attention."

Jennifer wasn't so sure. She looked back at Mitch lying on the cot, his face as white as the pillowcase. An uneasy feeling grew in the pit of her stomach. Maybe — just maybe — the eighth-graders had gotten in over their heads.

Steve Crowley had had it. He couldn't stand his class another second. He had decided to go AWOL, abdicate the throne, defect to another country. In other words, he was splitting.

Like some guy on a TV program who

says he's going down to the drugstore to buy a newspaper and then doesn't come back for six months, Steve abandoned his fourth-period class. Just walked out on them, after telling the little beasts he was stepping out to get a drink of water. His students acted like they never even heard him. They probably wouldn't even notice he was gone.

Steve didn't care. He wasn't going to waste any tears over *them*, either. It was such a relief to be out in the hall, away from those monsters disguised as seventh-graders. Steve felt a rush of admiration for any teacher brave enough to volunteer for junior high duty. He had never dreamed teaching would be so awful!

He passed Lucy Armanson's math class. Lucy was at the board, furiously jotting equations. Steve stopped to observe. Lucy's class actually seemed normal! No paper airplanes, no screaming kids. Was it because Lucy was teaching eighth-graders, who were naturally more mature and civilized? Yet a certain tenseness in Lucy's arm movements as she angrily chalked numbers across the board told Steve that all was definitely not well.

Then he looked back at her class. Every single student was asleep! They all had their heads down on their desks, like first-graders at naptime. Only one person sat upright: Mr. Geiger, the regular math teacher, attentively watching Lucy with a slightly amused expression on his face.

Steve went into her room, though he had vowed he would never willingly walk into another classroom as long as he lived, and tapped Lucy on the arm. She jumped.

"Steve Crowley! You scared the life out of me!"

"Well, I certainly couldn't scare the life out of *them*," he said. "What did you do to put them all asleep? Are you that boring, Lucy?"

Her black eyes snapped. "No, I'm not boring! I've done everything but stand on my head. I can't make them wake up. I can't make them do *anything*, much less learn math."

Another casualty, Steve thought, and a perfect candidate for his Drop-Out Club. "Ready to call it quits?"

Lucy rolled the chalk around in her palm, stalling. When she looked up at him again, her eyes were troubled. "I don't know. I'd like to walk out of here, but it's not right. We signed a contract."

"How about if we switch assignments? Not with each other, but ask for new ones," Steve suggested. "That's not quitting."

"But we're not supposed to," Lucy said. "Whatever job we got we have to stay with."

"Listen," Steven told her. "I was all for abiding by the rules, too. But this — " He indicated her passed-out class. "This is *ridiculous*. You aren't doing any good here."

"I know." Lucy bit her lip.

"I think we ought to go up to the office and tell Jason we want new assignments," Steve said.

"Who's going to take over our classes?"

A buzz of snores emanated from the front row.

"I don't think they really care," Steve said. "And my class is having a sort of unofficial study hall. Let's go. Our talents can be used elsewhere."

"Jason, if you don't *do* something, this school will be a pile of bricks by tomorrow," Jennifer insisted.

"What do you want me to do, Jennifer? Call out the National Guard? *One* kid gets hit by *one* stray medicine ball and you think it's a disaster. Stuff like that happens in schools every day. Even *our* school. Did you type that list of records for me? I'm stopping by the Record Shack after school."

"No, I did not type that list of records for you. We're not supposed to be doing personal business in the office."

"I'm in charge," Jason reminded her for about the forty-thousandth time that day.

"If things are a little slow, there's nothing wrong with doing some personal typing."

"Things *aren't* slow! It's a *madhouse* out there!" She stabbed her finger toward the plate glass windows where unauthorized students wandered around in the hall. "Why won't you go out and see for yourself? Don't take *my* word for it. Go down to the clinic and ask Mitch how slow things are in the boys' gym."

At that moment, Steve Crowley and Lucy Armanson came into the office. Jason looked at Steve and then back at Jennifer. "He'll do," he told Jennifer. "See, Miss Smarty? Decisions aren't so hard to make." He whirled and stalked back into his office, leaving Jennifer to do the dirty work, as usual.

"I'll do what?" Steve asked.

"Take over Mitch's class. Congratulations. You're the new boys' phys. ed. teacher," Jennifer informed him. "Got a crash helmet?"

Steve was only too glad to be rid of his seventh-grade geography classes. Jennifer arranged for his fourth-period class to go to the library. The rest of his classes would be subbed by some poor unfortunate eighth-grade recruit. Just so it wasn't him!

Steve had heard all about the so-called riot and Mitch's accident. But when he entered the gym, he saw no sign of an uprising. No strange ninth-grade giants. Sure, there were a few balls and towels lying around, but the gym looked like that all the time, until the coach yelled at them to straighten it up. Jennifer must have blown the whole thing out of proportion.

He went into the office next to the locker room and checked the clipboard. Fourth period — seventh-grade archery practice. Seventh-graders! He thought he was getting away from seventh-graders, but now he had to teach the blood-thirsty little monsters archery.

The locker room was empty, except for clothes strewn all over the benches. The class must already be dressed and out on the playing field. Steve grabbed the clipboard, an extra whistle, and ran outside. You couldn't trust seventh-graders alone for one *minute*, especially with bows and arrows in their grubby paws.

Surprisingly, his class was waiting for him on the edge of the playing field, bows and arrows in hand. A row of straw-filled targets had been set up against the hillside. Just over the hill was a patch of woods, dividing the school property from the back of a nearby housing development.

His class watched him approach. They seemed marvelously well-behaved.

Steve swallowed nervously.

Too well-behaved, just like that bunch he had in his first period class. . . . Alarmed, Steve studied the silent, grim group before him. They *were* the same — all the boys from that class, anyway. He was doomed. This was the same class that had set him on the path of no return. Only now they were armed.

"All right," he said in a quaking voice, "let's start practicing. First row. Face the targets . . . put your arrow to the string . . . pull back . . . aim . . . FIRE!"

They obeyed his commands, but the first volley of arrows zinged *over* the targets, sticking into the hillside. The second volley of arrows shot wildly into the air over the hill and into the field beyond. So did the third. And the fourth. Not one single archer managed to hit the *target*, much less the bull's-eye.

Volley after volley of arrows flew like birds into the hill, the field, even the woods.

When the bell rang, signaling the first lunch shift, the entire class flung their bows on the ground and ran into the school.

"Hey!" Steve shouted. "Come back here and pick up those arrows!" Of course they weren't coming back. Nothing could stop a herd of twelve-year-olds from going to lunch. And guess who was left to pick up all those hundreds of arrows scattered over half the countryside?

Chapter 12

"Places, everybody," Joan Wesley barked like a drill sergeant, pacing behind the steam tables.

They *were* in place, Nora felt like telling her. In place five whole minutes before the bell, waiting with plastic gloves on sweating hands, waiting with every muscle tensed.

Nora hoped most of the kids today had brought their lunch. If they hadn't, they'd be sorry.

"Smile!" Joan ordered. "You're performing a public service, girls."

"But this isn't the public," Nora said. "These are seventh-graders, not real people."

"Just look happy," Joan told her.

Nora crooked the corners of her mouth upward in what might pass as a smile and lifted the stainless-steel covers. Her smile dropped from her face.

"*What* is this?" she demanded as Joan swept by.

"It's meat loaf. Be sure and serve it with a smile!"

"I ought to serve it with a warning label from the surgeon general." Nora had never in her life *seen* more awful-looking stuff.

The first lunch shift bell jangled.

Wham! The double doors flew open with a bang and seventh-graders descended on the cafeteria like a plague of locusts.

Nora clenched her spoon tighter. As ready as she was, she'd never expected such an unruly mob. Did those kids act like that every day? She had nothing but the utmost sympathy for the ladies who regularly worked behind these steam tables.

Before the flood of seventh-graders reached their serving line, Nora reviewed the procedure once more with Tracy, who seemed to have slipped into a trance.

"Tracy! Pay attention! Now I put the meat loaf and rice on the plate, then hand it to you. You dish up the coleslaw in those little bowls and put that and a roll on each plate and hand it to the kid. Got that? We have to work fast, remember."

"Uh-huh." Tracy looked bored with the whole affair. Nora decided she'd wake up when the first kids came stampeding through their line.

Nora was not disappointed. The seventh-grade boys, pushing each other to be first in line, slammed metal trays on the rails, grabbed a handful of flatware, then positioned their trays before Nora.

"This all we got for dessert?" the first kid complained. "A crummy old cookie?"

Just be glad the bakers didn't bake them, Nora wanted to say. It had already been decided that prebaked butter cookies would be used today, instead of a fresh dessert.

"I bet it's stale," the other kid said. "And probably tastes like a dog biscuit."

Wait'll you get a taste of the meat loaf. Nora dished up a glob of the tomatoey mess and slapped it on the first kid's plate. How Mia managed to prepare liquid meat loaf was beyond her. At least the rice looked okay — if they had enough. She passed the plate across the counter to Tracy, then dished up the second kid's plate. When she slid that plate across, she heard a thunk — the second plate had crashed into the first plate. Tracy was off in Never-Never Land, while the plates were stacking up.

"Where's my lunch?" the first kid demanded. "How come you guys are so slow? I haven't got all day, you know."

Nora nudged Tracy. "Will you get moving?"

"Hurry up!" the second kid said in a surly tone.

Nora wanted to bean him over the head

with her ladle. The ungrateful children. Didn't they know she was doing the best she could?

Tracy spooned coleslaw into two little dishes. She picked up two rolls with her plastic-gloved hand and balanced them on the edge of the plates. One fell off. She picked it up and put it right on top of Mia's runny meat loaf before sliding the plate across the glass counter to the first boy.

He screamed as if he'd been shot. "You put my roll on that red stuff! Now it's all wet! I want another roll!"

Nora reached over and snatched the offending roll off the plate. "For heaven's sake," she snapped, plunking a fresh roll on Big Mouth's plate. "Move along — we've got other people to serve."

Behind those first two troublemakers was what appeared to be an unending stream of fiendish little faces.

Nora became an automaton. Dip, slap, dip, slap, pass. Over and over. Her right arm was killing her. She stood in one place so long, she felt her arches falling.

Joan Wesley patroled the serving lines like a prison warden, offering unwanted comments. "Speed it up," she told Tracy, a remark that bounced off Tracy like water rolling off a duck's back. "Act cheerful," she reminded Nora.

Nora was tempted to slug her with her spoon, too. How could anyone act cheerfully around these obnoxious clods? Nora had received nothing but abuse since the first two boys went through her line.

"What's this garbage?"

"I'm not eating that slop. It looks like it's poisoned!"

"I wish I'd gone to McDonald's!"

"Does that have tomatoes in it? I hate tomatoes. Gimme something else."

"What's that white stuff? It can't be rice. Rice is supposed to be fluffy, not all stuck together like glue."

"Hey, cafeteria lady. Can I have six cookies instead of meat loaf?"

And then there were the sound effects, mostly made by boys. Gagging motions, chokes, coughs, and assorted snorts. It took nerves of steel to work in a place like this, Nora decided.

After dishing up at least a million plates, the line trickled down to a few seventh-graders, and then nothing.

"Whew!" Nora sighed. "That's over with for a while. I wonder if we can rest."

"Rest, nothing!" Joan growled. "You girls get busy refilling those pans! The next lunch shift will start before you know it."

Nora gave in to temptation. She stuck her tongue out at Joan's retreating back.

Lucy came over and said to Tracy, "Let's trade places for a while. I think Mia's depressed over her meat loaf. The kids said some pretty awful things. Maybe you can cheer her up."

Tracy agreed and went over to Mia's side.

"I don't blame the kids," Nora said, lifting out an empty Main Dish tray so Lucy could put in a full one. "It looks horrible. I can just imagine how it must taste."

"It *is* a little runny." Lucy brought over a fresh pan of rolls. "These rolls don't look so hot, either."

"How can anybody make a runny meat loaf?" Nora asked. "No wonder the kids are revolting. Speaking of revolting, how come you're slumming down here?" she asked Lucy.

"I discovered I wasn't a very good math teacher," Lucy confessed. "So I became a free agent. Jennifer reassigned me to the kitchen, after Marcia left. It's not so bad here. At least nobody's asleep."

"Asleep!" Nora scoffed. "We haven't had one second to sit down, much less go to sleep."

Just then Amy Williams, the cafeteria monitor, came rushing into the serving area, her eyes round with panic.

"What's wrong?" Nora asked Amy. "Are the natives restless?"

"Worse!" Amy's breath came in ragged gasps. The front of her shirt was splotched with tomato sauce. "They're threatening a food fight!"

"A food fight!" Lucy exclaimed.

"They really hate the food," Amy said. "One kid hit another kid with a forkful of meat loaf. Now the whole table is talking about declaring war on all the other tables."

Nora couldn't picture Mia's meat loaf staying on the fork long enough to be lobbed at another person. It defied the laws of physics. "They'd better not throw around the rice," she said hotly. "Or my coleslaw. Not after I slaved all morning, grating and mixing — "

Lucy went to the doorway and peered out. "Uh-oh. I think it's starting! Amy, you'd better get back out there."

Amy shook her head. "I don't want to go! Do you know what it's like being the only eighth-grader in the midst of two hundred angry seventh-graders?"

"You can't hide in here." Lucy gave Amy a little push toward the door. "Go on. Show them you mean business. They'll settle down."

"Not after that meat loaf, they won't," Nora said gloomily.

The din from the lunchroom was incredible. Nora and Lucy and Amy looked at each other, waiting for a full-scale attack to erupt.

Miraculously, the bell rang. Two seconds later, the catcalls and jeering suddenly died. Nora ventured a peek into the cafeteria. The seventh-graders were meekly filing out the exit, leaving the scattered remains of their uneaten lunches like debris left in the wake of a tornado. The mighty ninth-graders had arrived, effectively averting a potential disaster.

"Get Tracy back over here before Wesley sees she's in the wrong line," Nora told Lucy. She would have gladly sacrificed Tracy's dubious help to have Lucy as a partner on the serving line, but Joan believed in running a strict kitchen.

Round Two began.

The ninth-graders didn't make obnoxious sounds or comments about the food like their predecessors. They had their own little game, Nora soon discovered. This shift raced their trays along the rails as if they were on their way to a fire.

"Hurry *up*! I got to meet my boyfriend."

"Will you make it snappy, girl?"

"Let's hustle back there. I'm starving!"

Nora ladled as fast as she could, feeling like a record that has been speeded up.

By the third shift, the eighth-grade lunch period, Nora was running short on smiles, cheerfulness, energy, patience — and rice.

"I knew we'd run out!" she cried when Tracy brought back the last pan with only a meager scraping of rice huddled in one corner. "What are we going to do?"

Tracy's eyes were glazed over. She was tired, too. "Let's not do anything. Just pretend this is all they're supposed to get."

Nora wasn't crazy about the idea, but she had no alternative. Without the rice to help cover up and absorb Mia's meat loaf, the main course looked soupier and more unappetizing than ever.

The eighth-graders didn't seem to care. Members of Nora's class slogged through the line like zombies. She recognized the cafeteria monitors by their food-spattered clothes. Halfway through the line she saw Jennifer.

"Jennifer!" Nora leaned across the counter. "Take my advice and don't touch the meat loaf. Only the coleslaw is edible. You got any granola bars in your locker? I'd eat those, if I were you."

"Nora, you should see your hair. It's so curly! I wish I could get my hair that curly. I need two plates, by the way."

"Just stick your head over a steam table for two hours," Nora said, noting that her best friend looked as neat as she had that morning. "It'll frizz like crazy. Who's the other plate for?"

"Jason. Who else?"

"What's the matter? Is his Highness too good to be seen groveling in the lunchroom with the rest of the peasants?" Nora gave Jason's plate an extra-big helping of meat loaf, out of spite.

Jennifer sighed. "He won't come out of the office, Nora. Not even to eat lunch. You ought to see what's going *on* out there. A riot in the gym. The clinic is a disaster. I've tried and tried to tell him, but he goes right on believing things are hunky-dory."

"I don't know whose idea it was to run the school for a day, but it sure was a rotten one."

"Nora! It was *your* idea. Don't you remember?"

"I can barely remember my own *name*."

"Only a few hours to go. Take care, Nora." Jennifer took the plates and moved on down the line.

Nora became a machine again. Dip, splat, dip, splat. The line wound around the cafeteria wall, endless.

"Hey, Nora!" She looked up to see Jim Blake, a friend of Steve's. "What's that junk you're serving? Doesn't look very nutritious."

Nutritious! If he only *knew* what she had been through in order to put food on his plate! And he had the nerve to complain that it didn't look very nutritious! For the first time in her life, Nora couldn't care less about other people's diets. If she had *her* way, she'd stand on a stool in the middle of the cafeteria, with a hundred cooling fans blowing on her, and throw the school bags of taco chips and packages of those dreadful cupcakes with the cold cream fillings inside. Give them what they truly deserve.

"Hi, Nora," drawled a familiar voice near the end of the line. It was Marc Johnson, pushing a tray and grinning his lazy smile. "Working hard or hardly working?" he quipped. Nora's self-control, stretched to the limit, was in danger of snapping.

"What do you want, Marc?" she said. "We're out of rice, rolls, cookies, coleslaw, clean silverware, and napkins. All we have is meat loaf, though I can't really recommend it."

"Why not? It looks great. Give me a plateful," he said eagerly.

Another myth toppled! And to think she believed Marc was into a healthy life-style. She piled his plate high with Mia's disgusting meat loaf. He took it happily.

When the bell rang and the eighth-graders left for fifth period, Joan announced it was the workers turn to eat.

"Eat *what*?" Nora asked.

Joan uncovered yet another pan of meat loaf. "We've got plenty of main dish left," she said.

Nora pretended to swoon. "Mia's meat loaf! I can't stand it! That stuff multiplies!"

"Like something out of a horror movie," Lucy agreed. She found two clean pot lids, since they had run out of plates. "Here, we can put our food on these. What'll you have, Nora? The chef's special, meat loaf a la king? Or would you care for meat loaf with meat loaf sauce? Or how about meat loaf with meatballs?"

"Oh, be quiet," Nora said.

Chapter 13

The eighth-grade lunch shift bell rang, but Denise Hendrix did not dare leave the clinic. How could she, with an infirmary full of patients? Only two seventh-grade boys had left for lunch — the rest remained in the clinic, steadfastly clinging to their stomachaches, headaches, bruises, and cut fingers.

"Aren't you hungry?" Denise asked Susan Hillard, hoping Susan would leave for lunch and take some of the boys with her.

"Don't make me gag," Susan said, each word weighted with disgust. "If you had seen those sinks I was supposed to clean — " She closed her eyes to shut out the horrible memory.

No one was budging, Denise realized. They were staying put until *she* treated them. She couldn't handle this — it was way too much responsibility.

From the cot, Mitch struggled to sit up. "Giant ninth-graders . . ." he murmured. "Ninth-graders from outer space. Are they still in my gym?"

Genuine fear rippled down Denise's spine. Mitch must be delirious, babbling about giant ninth-graders from outer space! He really needed attention. The bump on his head seemed to have gone down, but she couldn't be sure.

"Mitch?" she asked tentatively. "How do you feel?"

"Awful." He fell back against the pillows. "Those guys must have been ten feet tall. They ran right over me. Like I wasn't even there."

"Don't talk, Mitch. Just rest." Denise couldn't stand to hear him go on about giant ninth-graders.

What should she do for him? Take his temperature? Raise his head? Raise his feet? Lower his head? No, that was the same thing — or was it? Her brain felt clogged. She had once taken a first-aid course in Europe, but that had been years ago and she hadn't really listened to the instructor.

Mrs. Haggerty placidly knitted away, totally unaware that her substitute was dying a thousand deaths. How could the woman sit there like Whistler's Mother, never even dropping a stitch, with all the groaning going on around her?

"Mrs. Haggerty," Denise began.

"Yes, Nurse Hendrix?" Mrs. Haggerty said.

Denise winced. For all practical purposes, she *was* the nurse on duty, as much as she hated to hear it. Except in extreme emergencies, Denise was supposed to run this clinic by herself. What constituted an extreme emergency, anyway? Bleeding to death? A broken leg?

She looked over at Mitch Pauley. He didn't *seem* very sick, except for those strange remarks about giant ninth-graders. He certainly wasn't bleeding to death. Could he have broken his head bone when he fell?

"Mrs. Haggerty, I'm not sure what to do for Mitch."

The older nurse finished the row she was knitting before answering. "Well, Nurse Hendrix. What do you think you *should* do?"

"I — I suppose I should examine his head," Denise stammered. What she ought to do is have her *own* head examined for taking this assignment in the first place!

"Well, then, why don't you?" the nurse asked mildly.

Why didn't she? Because she didn't

know what to look for. Denise bent over the cot, feeling hopelessly inadequate. If something happened to Mitch, it would be *her* fault, no one else's.

Jennifer Mann came into the clinic, tripping over four boys sitting on the floor. "Good grief," she said to Denise. "I thought some of these idiots would have gone to lunch. Isn't anybody hungry?"

"I'm not," Denise said. Food was the last thing on her mind.

"Don't mention food," Susan moaned. "I may never eat again."

"To tell you the truth, you didn't miss much," Jennifer admitted. "I came in here to check on Mitch. How's he doing?"

Denise clutched Jennifer's arm like a life preserver. "Jennifer, thank heavens you're here. I need help. I don't know how Mitch is doing."

"What do you mean?"

"I mean, I don't know what to *do* for him. Nurse Haggerty says to examine him, but I don't know what to look for. He has a big bump on his head. That's all I know."

"But you're the nurse," Jennifer insisted.

"I'm *not* a nurse! I've never had any training! Jennifer, I haven't done *one* single thing right since I took over the clinic this morning. Putting a Band-Aid on the wrong finger is one thing — but this is something else. This is *serious*!"

Jennifer thought for a second. "You're right. This *is* serious. If you don't know what to do for Mitch, I know somebody who will. Nora."

"Nora! Of course! She's always talking about medical stuff." Denise nearly fainted with relief. Nora Ryan, who wanted to be a doctor more than anything in the world, was her answer.

"She's on kitchen duty," Jennifer said. "I'll go get her."

"Me, too." Denise turned to Susan and made her second decision of the day. "Jennifer and I are going to get help for Mitch. I'm leaving you in charge."

"Me!" Susan shrieked. "I'm one of the patients! You can't run out on us. Denise, get back here! Denise!"

With lunch over at long last, Nora thought she'd sit down and put her feet up while the others finished up. If she could just find a nice soft couch, she'd lie down and never move —

"Wrong," Joan Wesley informed her. "You and Tracy have to scrub all the pots and pans and utensils you used today."

"Why?" Nora bellowed, furious at having her nice soft couch shot out from under her. "What about the dishwashers? How come they don't wash the pans?"

"They have to wash six hundred plates and bowls and all that flatware," Joan replied. "Even with the dishwashing machine, it'll take them all afternoon."

Nora stamped over to her station. There were *hundreds* of those enormous stainless-steel pans heaped in the sink. And no Tracy, naturally. Where had that girl disappeared to *now*?

She finally found Tracy in the furnace room, behind a hot water tank with Marc Johnson, reading one of Marc's comic books.

It was hard to decide which of the two of them was the most worthless. She gave up on Marc, but she still needed Tracy.

Nora prodded her partner all the way back to their station.

While Tracy filled the sink with hot sudsy water, Nora sorted the pans. There were eight sticky rice pans, six coleslaw pans, the two onion pans, and a mountain of other bowls and pots they had used to scoop up the avalanche of rice.

"I'll wash," Nora said. "You dry." The pans, which seemed to have grown to the size of Volkswagens, were too big to fit in the sink. Nora angled one down into the hot soapy water, like a sliding board.

Nora looked up to see Jennifer and Denise.

"Jennifer! What are you doing here? Bringing another special request from King Jason? What's he want now — Beef Wellington and baked Alaska?"

"Nora, we need your help," Jennifer said urgently. "It's Mitch Pauley. He was hit on the head in gym a little while ago. We took him to the clinic, but Denise doesn't know what to do for him."

Nora shifted her attention to Denise, who looked pale and sick herself. "Where was he hit?"

"On the forehead." Denise indicated the spot on her own forehead.

"Is he conscious? Talking?" Jennifer and Denise both nodded. "When he speaks, is he coherent, logical?" Nora pursued.

"He keeps talking about those giant ninth-graders," Denise said. "Really weird."

"He could have a concussion," Nora concluded. "Of course, I haven't seen him, so I don't really know."

"Will you come back with us and look at him?" Denise pleaded.

Nora wiped her wet hands on her food-smeared apron, then took it off and threw it on the bakers' pastry board. She hurried out with Jennifer and Denise.

"Ryan, where are you going!" Joan Wesley's drill sergeant bark followed her out the door. "You're not finished!"

"Oh, yes, I am!" Nora said gleefully.

They cut through the cafeteria, which looked like a bomb site. Napkins and straw wrappers everywhere. Chairs overturned, Nora skidded in a patch of coleslaw. The floor was covered with mashed food, food that *she* had worked her fingers to the bone preparing.

After the grim prison of the kitchen, the hallways were like a carnival. Nora was shocked at the way kids ran like animals through the halls and shouted in the classrooms. The last day of school wasn't this wild.

"Has it been like this all day?" she asked Jennifer.

Jennifer nodded. "In some places it's even worse. Down by industrial arts it's practically a war zone. You need a bodyguard to go down that hall."

"What disciplinary measures has Jason taken?" Nora asked, borrowing a phrase she'd heard the principal use. "What's he *doing* about it?"

Jennifer's answer was short and to the point. "Nothing."

Nora was appalled at the number of boys hanging out around the infirmary.

Only Denise could attract that many males, all willing to risk losing a limb just to be in the same room with her.

Nora elbowed her way to the cot. "Hi, Mitch. How're you feeling?"

"Hey, Nora," he said. "Is it time to go home yet?"

Nora sighed. When Denise walked into a room, boys forgot about eating lunch. When *she* came into a room, boys suddenly remembered they had other things to do, like go home. She looked at Mitch's bump. It was a doozy, all right. Purplish and huge, like one of the ugly dahlias in her neighbor's garden.

"Mitch, what is your mother's maiden name?" she asked him. Emergency room doctors usually asked that question when someone was brought in with a head injury.

"What?" Mitch stared at her.

"Never mind. Does your head hurt?"

"Of course, it hurts! How stupid can you get?"

Now what? Nora knew that doctors sometimes flashed a penlight into the eyes of the victim, but what were they looking for? A head injury needed professional care.

"Well?" Denise prompted, clearly waiting for Nora to perform a miracle cure.

"It's no use," Nora said sadly. "We don't

know what we're doing here." She appealed to Nurse Haggerty. "Will you look at him? Please?"

"Of course," the nurse said, coming over. "I've been waiting for Miss Hendrix to ask me. I think I would have given up hours ago, if I had been in her shoes." She smiled at Denise. "Don't worry, child. I wouldn't have let you treat someone improperly."

"But what about Mitch?" Denise asked. "He could really be hurt and I haven't done anything."

Mrs. Haggerty examined Mitch's bump with strong, sure fingers. "Mr. Pauley is going to be fine," she pronounced. "He has a nasty bump, but the swelling is already starting to go down. I'll give him an ice pack. Unless you want to do the honors."

"Yeah, yeah!" Mitch urged. He wasn't *too* sick, Nora thought.

Denise backed away. "You go ahead. I think — I think I'll go get some air."

She left the clinic, a flock of boys trailing after her.

"What are you going to do now?" Jennifer asked. "Are you going back to the kitchen?"

"Not on your life. I left behind a stack of pans as tall as the Sears building." Nora wouldn't go back to that ghastly place unless she were horsewhipped. Maybe not even then.

A mob of seventh-grade girls, singing the school song at the top of their lungs, ran past, nearly knocking Nora over. She looked at Jennifer. "This isn't working, Jen. If Jason doesn't do something, the governor's going to call in the troops."

"I've told Jason about the conditions out here till I'm blue in the face, but he just won't listen. Will you come back to the office with me? Maybe you can talk some sense into him."

Nora and Jennifer battled their way to the office, shutting the sound-proof door behind them. They could still see the boiling mass of kids in the hall outside the windows, but at least they were spared hearing the racket.

Tommy Ryder was sitting at Jennifer's desk, pecking at the typewriter. He looked frayed at the edges, like the last pair of jeans on a bargain table, Nora thought. He didn't even flash his famous grin.

"What are you typing?" Jennifer asked.

"My resignation. I quit. Get yourself another guidance counselor." He ripped the page from the typewriter, tearing it in half as he did so. "Four weepy girls camped in my office today. I can't take another one."

"You can't quit either," Jennifer told him. "Those students out there need guidance."

Tommy taped together the two halves of the paper with the jerky motions of someone who had to catch a plane. "Guidance! Are you joking? By the way, there's a mess in my office. I mean, Mrs. Fauconnet's office."

"What kind of a mess? Susan Hillard's out of commission," Jennifer reminded him.

"Five million soggy tissues and maybe a leftover bawling girl." He handed Jennifer his taped-together resignation. "I gotta get out of here. Give this to Jason."

"That's not all we're going to give Jason," Nora said, curling her right hand into a fist. "I'd like to give him a piece of my mind! Jason has practically *ruined* the whole project by letting this happen! The school will never let us live this down. The eighth-graders are the laughing stock of Cedar Groves!"

"I agree," said Jennifer. "Enough's enough. Let's go in there after him." She walked over to the principal's private office. The door was closed. Outside, on the floor, was an untouched lunch tray.

Jennifer rattled the doorknob.

"What's wrong?" Nora asked.

"It's locked." Jennifer said. "Our fearless leader has locked himself in his office!"

Chapter 14

"Locked! It can't be locked. Let me try." Nora wrung the doorknob, but it didn't turn. Jennifer was right. Jason Anthony, their principal-for-a-day, had locked himself inside his office.

Nora banged on the door. "Jason, open this door! Do you hear me? Open the door!"

"It's no use," Jennifer said. "He's locked himself in and he's not coming out."

"He could at least *answer* us," Nora said, indignantly. "Jason! You twerp! Get out here and take it like the rest of us!"

No reply. It was as if they were yelling in a hollow tree.

Jennifer pushed her hair behind her ears. "Why won't he answer?"

"Because he's *scared*, that's why. The big coward," Nora said scathingly. "What happened to the smart-aleck saluting the buses this morning? He was all gung-ho to take over as principal. But then he found out the job was too much for him so he ducked out."

"The job *is* too much," Jennifer pointed out quietly. "Not just for Jason, but for all of us."

Nora hated to admit defeat, but she had to agree. "I think we bit off more than we could chew. But we can't quit! We have to see it through to the end. If we give up now, we'll never have a voice in this school ever again. Don't you see?"

"I admire your dedication," Jennifer said, loyal as ever. "Especially after you spent a grueling day in the kitchen. You've worked harder than any of us. But, Nora, too many of us have *already* given up and walked off the job. Tommy. Susan. Denise. Lucy and Steve quit teaching, though they took other assignments. I bet we couldn't *pay* those kids to go back."

"Which is why we need Jason," Nora maintained staunchly. "He *is* our leader, such as he is. It's up to him to set the example and pull us back together. Let's face it, Jen, if word leaks out that the principal has gone into hiding, we'll never gain control of this school."

Jennifer glanced nervously out the office windows where hostile-looking seventh-graders leered at them. "What you say makes sense, but all the logic in the world won't make those kids behave. They're absolutely rabid. We'll never get them to settle down."

"Only the seventh-graders are running berserk," Nora observed. "If we get the ninth-graders to cooperate, they'll sit on the little kids." Nora sounded confident but she was nervous, too. She knew what had to be done, but *getting* it done was another story. If the eighth-grade class blew it today —

Steve Crowley straggled into the office. Nora and Jennifer stared at him. The knees of his pants were grimy with dirt. Burrs clung to his jacket.

"What happened to *you*?" Jennifer demanded.

"Don't ask," he replied. "I've been subbing for Mitch, teaching archery."

"On your hands and knees? I thought you were supposed to use a bow and arrow."

"Very funny." Steve raked his hands through his brown hair, dislodging a nest of twigs and leaves. "You might be interested to know, *Miss Ryan*, since you are responsible for this whole disastrous day, that the ninth-graders are staging a strike."

"I was hoping nobody would remember it was my idea," Nora muttered.

"Strike?" Jennifer echoed. "What kind of a strike?"

"A walk-out," Steve replied. "And there they go." He waved a grass-stained hand at the windows. Sure enough, squadrons of ninth-graders paraded by the office, boldly heading for the front doors.

"They can't leave!" Nora screeched. "The last bell hasn't rung yet. We'll get in trouble if they walk out! We're responsible!"

"I've got news for you," Steve told her. "We were in trouble from the minute we took over the school this morning."

"Jason has to order those kids back inside. It's the only way," Nora said.

Steve looked around the office. "Where is General MacArthur, anyway?"

"Locked in the principal's office. He won't open the door or even answer us," Jennifer said.

Nora steered Steve over to Jason's office. "We have to get him out. You bust down the door."

"I can't break down the principal's door! Mr. Donovan will expel me!"

"This is an *emergency*," Nora persisted. "If we don't get our school under control soon, we'll all be packed off to reform school!"

Just then Lucy and Mia sprinted into the office, flinging themselves in a heap on the visitor's couch.

"Are you okay?" Jennifer asked them. "What happened?"

Lucy was the first to catch her breath. "It's a jungle out there! We ran all the way from the cafeteria."

"I never thought I'd feel safe in the office!" Mia still wore her meat loaf-spattered apron and hairnet. Her purple-streaked hair, stuffed in the unflattering hairnet and limp from hours over a steam table, sat on her head like a soggy blueberry pancake. Mia did not look very punk. In fact, she looked as if she'd sailed around the world in a teacup, Nora thought.

"Have any of you guys seen Andy?" Mia asked. "I looked for him in the biology lab but all I saw was this incredible mess. Papers all over the place. I think somebody let the gerbils loose."

"More like somebody let the seventh-graders loose," Nora said.

"Maybe Andy is hiding out with Jason," Steve said.

The striking ninth-graders marched past the office windows like rats deserting a sinking ship. In the background, the seventh-graders were cheering them on, no doubt eager to be rid of the upperclassmen so they could overthrow the beseiged opposition, the feeble eighth-graders.

"There's only one thing to do," Nora

said, going back to her original plan. "Break the door down and drag Jason out. With all of us, we ought to be able to do it." She arranged the five of them into a human battering-ram. "On the count of three — Ready? One . . . two . . . three!"

They hurled themselves against the door, getting in each other's way and falling into each other. The door didn't give an inch.

Nora rubbed her sore shoulder. "We need to put the muscle up front. This time Steve ought to be over here and — "

"I don't think that will be necessary," came a firm voice. Mr. Donovan, the principal — the *real* principal — stood behind them. Mrs. Peters had reclaimed her desk. The rest of the administrative staff were filtering back to their regular places.

Mr. Donovan stared at them, his arms folded across his chest. He looked so businesslike, so grown-up, so authoritative. He was like the cavalry, arriving in the nick of time.

"Mr. Donovan!" Nora cried. "We were just — "

"I've got eyes," he said grimly. He did not look happy. "I can see you were attempting to break my door down."

"For a good reason," Jennifer said quickly. "Jason's in there. And he won't come out."

"The ninth-graders are on strike," Steve filled in. "They're leaving the school. We have to get Jason to — " His sentence faded away.

Nora felt a rush of anger at both of them. Boy, they couldn't wait to deliver the bad news! "But we were getting things under control," she hastened to explain.

"I can see that, too," Mr. Donovan said, every syllable crisp with sarcasm. "I'll take over now, if you don't mind."

He flicked the switch of the P.A. microphone sitting on the counter. In a no-nonsense tone he announced that the eighth-grade "reign" of Cedar Groves Junior High was hereby at an end and all students were to report to their regular sixth-period classrooms where they belonged, *without delay* or he would start handing out suspension slips.

His voice booming out of the loudspeakers had an amazing effect. The ninth-graders on their way out the front door wheeled, making a sharp about-face. The rollicking seventh-graders disbanded and headed in the direction of their rooms, with only a few scattered murmurs of protest.

"Now I'll attend to this little matter." Mr. Donovan took a key from his pocket and unlocked the door to his office. "Jason Anthony. Come out here immediately, young man, unless you want twenty demerits."

Jason came out, grinning sheepishly. "Hi there, Mr. Donovan," he said. "Is the school day over?"

"It is for you," Mr. Donovan said.

"Way to go, Jason," Nora said. "Leaving us to take the heat."

"Whatever are you talking about?" Jason raised his eyebrows, the picture of innocence.

"You know exactly what I'm talking about. Locking yourself in there — not answering anybody."

"Oh, was somebody calling me? I was on the floor looking for a paper clip," Jason said blithely. "I guess I didn't hear you."

"I suppose the wind blew your door shut and locked it?" Nora accused.

"These things do happen." Jason regained his composure faster than anyone Nora knew. He went over and shook Mr. Donovan's hand. "It was a pleasure replacing you, sir. Feel free to call on me any time." He gave Nora and the others a little salute as he passed. "As you were, troops."

Nora was incredulous. "Can you *believe* that guy?"

"I can't believe this whole day," Mr. Donovan said, more to himself than to them. "Which, as I announced, is over. You all can go now."

Nora could practically see relief spread through the others. But she wasn't ready to throw in the towel just yet. "Mr. Donovan, we signed an agreement that we're supposed to work the whole school day. It's only — "

Mr. Donovan cut her off with an impatient gesture. "Is this how you kids fulfill your agreement, Nora? Are you at your posts?"

Now it was Nora's turn to look sheepish. "No, sir, we're not. Except for Jennifer."

"Well, then, it seems to me the experiment has been over for quite some time."

"Yes, sir." Nora was woefully aware how bedraggled they looked. They had failed. The eighth grade would never have a say at Cedar Groves Junior High as long as the building stood on this foundation. And it was all her fault.

Mr. Donovan's stern face split into an unexpected smile. "Perhaps things did not go as — er, smoothly as you planned. But I admire your spirit."

What spirit? Nora wondered. Except for Jason, they looked like people who had spent the last month in a foxhole.

"Nora, your class has worked very hard today to make a point," the principal went on. "You wanted certain things changed at Cedar Groves and you tried to change them yourselves. Such enthusiasm should not go unrewarded."

For a horrible instant Nora thought he was going to let them run the school forever.

"We — the faculty, the staff, and myself — are willing to listen to your side," he said. "We will sit down with representatives from your class and try to come to a compromise. How's that?"

Nora glanced at the others in her group. The day was not a total loss after all! "Fine, sir. We appreciate it."

"Good." The principal turned back to the microphone.

"Attention, everyone. All eighth-grade substitutes still at their posts are dismissed. Please return to your regular sixth-period class. Tomorrow we resume our regular, *normal* schedule."

Nora and Jennifer exchanged a grateful glance. It *was* over, finally.

Before signing off for the day, Mr. Donovan added mysteriously, with just a hint of a smile, "I would like to thank a 'special group' out there for their efforts in making this day a success. You *know* who you are."

He shut off the microphone again and

began issuing orders to the office staff to go out and round up any stray ninth-graders who were still trying to skip class.

Nora and Jennifer left the office. Lucy, Steve, and Mia fell in step with them.

"I still can't believe it's over," Nora said, feeling as though she had just been released from jail.

"What do you think Mr. Donovan meant by 'special group'?" Lucy wanted to know.

Steve kicked at a pile of trash. The janitors, the real ones, were going to have to work overtime to clean up the mess. "He meant us, naturally. After all, *some*body ought to thank us for what we did today."

"But he was *looking* at those teachers and the others in the office when he said that," Jennifer said. "You don't suppose he's going to tell our teachers to give us an extra-rough time from now on, do you?"

Lucy gave Jennifer a harmless slap. "Perish the thought."

"They could," Steve said. "To get even with us for the Gripe Revolution and everything."

"You know," Nora said. "Some very strange things happened here today."

"Yeah, we ran the school," Lucy said. "And I for one am glad it's over!"

"Aside from that." Nora stopped, forcing the others to stop, too. She ticked off the events on her fingers. "First, there were all those boys in the clinic. And then there was the riot in the gym — "

"Those gigantic ninth-graders!" Jennifer cried. "They couldn't have been from our school. At least I don't *think* they were."

Steve was dubious. "Nobody saw those guys except you and Mitch."

"And look what happened to *him*," Jennifer said defensively.

Nora continued tallying up odd incidents. "We almost had a food fight — "

"And Tommy kept having girls come into his office and start crying," Jennifer said. "I wonder why they did that — it was obviously a put-on."

"Talk about strange," Steve said. "My first-period geography class never said a word, but they had this whole scam designed to drive a teacher over the edge. It worked, too. Then I got the same class for archery, and they shot their arrows all over the school grounds, and I had to pick them up."

"My math classes!" Lucy chimed in. "Disasters! Nobody came prepared. And they had the most ridiculous excuses you ever heard. One class even fell asleep."

Nora shook her head. "Do you suppose the regular staff goes through this all the

time? I mean, how do they *cope*? How do the cafeteria ladies manage to get lunch ready on time every single day, never mind what it tastes like?"

"Teaching isn't the piece of cake I thought it was, either," Steve said. "I'm amazed our teachers can get us to sit *down*, much less teach us anything."

"And Mrs. Haggerty," Lucy added. "She doesn't go off the deep end when there is an emergency the way Denise did."

"I'll never grumble about how slow Mrs. Peters is in the office," Jennifer declared. "Sometimes I have to wait for her to write me out a late pass. Now I know what she's *doing* behind that counter — answering phones, typing, making appointments for guidance counselors. All at once!"

"Running a school isn't what it's cracked up to be," Mia concluded with a sigh.

"It might be if we'd had some experience," Jennifer said. "When I think it over, those giant ninth-graders only *seemed* big because they were a whole year more grown-up than we are."

"Even the seventh-graders look like giants to me," Nora said dismally. "I'm just worn out." The others murmured in agreement.

Yet of the five of them, Jennifer seemed the least frazzled, Nora thought. Whenever there had been a crisis, Jennifer was right there, handling it. Maybe she didn't need lessons in self-confidence, after all.

Just then the bell rang, signaling the end of sixth period and the end of the longest day any of them could remember.

"It's over," Mia said wearily. "I'm going to find Andy and go home. I sure hope my mother isn't having meat loaf tonight."

There was the usual insanity as classes dispersed and kids raced through the halls, slamming lockers, calling out to their friends. Nora and Jennifer allowed themselves to be carried along by the tide of students rushing to the buses lined up at the curb.

Outside, the cold air hit Nora like a bucket of water. Trapped in a hot, steamy kitchen most of the day, she had almost forgotten what fresh air felt like. Along with the blast of chilly air came a feeling of intense exhaustion. She could hardly lift her feet—it was as if she had flatirons tied to her shoes.

Marc Johnson loped along beside Nora. He didn't appear the slightest bit tired, but then why should he? Seeing Marc made Nora think of cabbage and onions, not a very romantic combination. He was one boy she could forget easily. In fact, she didn't know what she ever saw in him in the first place.

They staggered out to the bus. Jennifer found them a seat near the back. Nora plopped into it like a sack of coal. She noticed a vaguely familiar sheet of paper sticking out of Jennifer's notebook.

"What's that?"

Jennifer pulled out the paper. "Our Gripe List. What do you want me to do with it?"

"Burn it," she said.

Steve and Mitch Pauley stumbled into the seat across from them. Mitch's forehead was bruised, but otherwise he looked fine. On the lawn outside, Mr. Donovan was taking down the flags. Nora remembered how Jason had stood by the flagpole this morning, saluting the buses. She also remembered her own excitement for the project that had been her idea, distantly, like recalling the thrill of her first birthday party.

"Who do you suppose will be on the committee to meet with the principal?" Jennifer asked.

Nora was too tired to reply. All she wanted was to soak her aching bones in a hot tub for about twenty-seven hours. And then she wanted to lie down on a soft bed for another twenty-seven hours.

Tomorrow was another school day. It would be such a *relief* to get back to their dull, boring routine. If she lived through the night, Nora knew she'd never complain about a single thing in their school ever again.

One final thought managed to squeeze its way out of her exhausted brain. Maybe Jennifer was right. It was possible things had gone wrong today because running a school *was* a tough job. Too tough for inexperienced, unprepared eighth-graders. She wondered if she should volunteer to be one of the representatives from their class. After all, she had experience now. There wasn't anything she didn't know about making coleslaw for six hundred.

When she was fully recovered, Nora decided, she'd call Jennifer and ask her if this day really and truly happened.

Why does Nora suddenly feel like life was easier in seventh grade? Read Junior High #4, HOW DUMB CAN YOU GET?